RIDERS IN THE STORM

It was 1899 and the winter in Montana was brutal. Ed Cotton had no idea what the sheriff wanted when he rode up to his door. But Deputy Sheriff Fred Rome arrested Cotton for a murder he hadn't committed. He'd been framed but nobody knew who had done it. It was up to his best girl and his best friend to find out who was behind it— and why.

RIDERS IN THE STORM

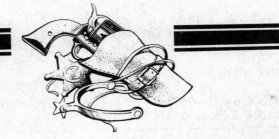

Lee Floren

ATLANTIC LARGE PRINT

Chivers Press, Bath, England.
Curley Publishing, Inc.,
South Yarmouth, Mass., USA.

Library of Congress Cataloging in Publication Data

Floren, Lee.
  Riders in the storm/Lee Floren.
    p. cm.—(Atlantic large print)
  ISBN 1–55504–949–4 (lg. print)
  1. Large type books.   I. Title.
[PS3511.L697R53 1989]
813'.52—dc20

89–1488
CIP

British Library Cataloguing in Publication Data

Floren, Lee, *1910–*
  Riders in the storm. (Atlantic large print.
  Chivers Atlantic western large print)
  I. Title
  813'.52(F)

  ISBN 0–7451–9552–0
  ISBN 0–7451–9564–4

This Large Print edition is published by Chivers Press, England, and
Curley Publishing, Inc, U.S.A. 1989

Published by arrangement with Donald MacCampbell, Inc

U.K. Hardback ISBN 0 7451 9552 0
U.K. Softback ISBN 0 7451 9564 4
U.S.A. Softback ISBN 1 55504 949 4

RIDERS IN THE STORM

CHAPTER ONE

Winter had come early in September to this Montana high country in the year of 1899. Now it was almost Christmas time, and Ed Cotton was a cowboy on foot trying to string barbed wire in the cold. He was angry with himself and the cold weather.

He was angry because he had become a homesteader. He was angry at the snow god because he had pushed winter on to this snow-covered range.

Ed was stringing wire on the south side of his homestead. He was fighting the balky wire, which was cold and ornery. He had the spool tied to the back of his wagon, and when he drove his team ahead, the wire should have unrolled easily behind him. But it tangled and snarled up, and now Ed was on foot attempting to straighten it so he could drive ahead again.

He cursed under his breath.

Ed Cotton was twenty-four and he had red hair. He was bony almost to the point of being gaunt, and he stood an inch over six feet. Wind and storm had marked his face with its high cheekbones, and wind and storm had given him a look older than his years.

His temper matched his flaming red hair, and his stubbornness was equal to his flaring

1

temper. Now his breath hung on the cold air. The thermometer stood at eight below zero. The cold sunlight, slanting off the banks of new snow, lighted the planes of his dark face. He wore a heavy overcoat and overshoes, and his heavy mittens—cowhide mittens with woollen liners—protected his hands from the cold and the spines of the barbed wire.

His team stood hip-humped, waiting for him to climb into the high spring seat and drive on, the barbed wire stringing out behind the wagon. Back of the team, about a hundred yards away, was the cabin and barn, set against the slope of a rocky hill that had a spring that ran all the year around. He had already set the diamond-willow posts, and for that he was thankful. A man could not punch postholes through snow, with the ground freezing underneath to icy flint.

Nobody but a fool, he thought, would fence in this kind of weather. Nobody but a fool, or a man who wanted to get his homestead under barbed wire before winter really set in.

Suddenly he heard horses approaching.

He looked up, startled, for he had figured he was alone. His homestead was some distance from the road that ran from the Triangle Diamond, the biggest spread in that section, to the cow town of Greener, about five miles away. Therefore surprise showed momentarily on his frost-pinched face as he watched the two riders lope toward him. Then he recognized them.

One was Deputy Sheriff Fred Rome. Rome headed the pair, riding a sorrel gelding—a powerful animal with thick shoulders and barrel. Ed Cotton put his gaze on the second rider. For a while he could not recognize him; then as they came closer, he recognized this rider as Cart Nagle.

What was this pair doing so far off the beaten trail?

For some reason, Ed Cotton had a premonition of danger, and the weight of his .45 under his mackinaw was a welcome burden. He stood there and waited for the pair to ride in, and he beat his mittened hands together to keep blood moving through him.

Then the pair pulled in. They both wore angora chaps and overshoes and overcoats, and both, he noticed, had their guns strapped over their coats. This told him they rode on important business.

Their horses were sweating despite the cold, and their breathing was heavy. Ed's fears crystallized as he spoke slowly.

'You two must be on an important bit of business, seein' you rid so fast an' so far in this cold weather. Winter sure boomed down on us in a hurry, huh?'

Deputy Sheriff Fred Rome was about five feet seven, squat and powerful. He had a wide beefy face, marked by fine red lines, and he liked fast company and the bottle. He wore a Stetson hat, and he had a bandanna under it, tied around his face to keep his ears from freezing. The knot under his thick jaw moved as he spoke.

'This is the end of our trail, Nagle.'

Cart Nagle was the direct opposite of the deputy. He was a slender man of about thirty-five or forty, and he was a gambler. He hung around the El Dorado down in Greener, where he gambled and sometimes tended bar. He had a long nose, blue now from the cold, and this nose was flanked by two sombre eyes.

'This looks like it, Rome,' the gambler's thin lips said.

Ed Cotton did not like either of these men. Fred Rome, in his estimation, was a big blustering devil, arrogant with the authority of his badge. Cart Nagle, on the other hand, was too quiet, too secretive and too sly. Ed held him in silent dislike also because he schemed and planned how to get money from honest, hardworking cowpunchers. He disliked him with the dislike an outdoor man has for an indoor man. Now he felt anger stir through him.

Ed's voice was sharp. 'Stop talkin' aroun' the corner, Rome. What's this all about?'

'You're under arrest, Cotton!' Rome said huskily.

Ed knew surprise. But he kept his face

expressionless and his temper down.

'Me under arrest? What's the charge, Rome?'

'Murder!'

Ed stared at the deputy sheriff. But the man's heavy face was serious. His grey eyes moved over and met the flat eyes of Cart Nagle. This pair, he realized, was serious.

And *murder* was an ugly word.

'Me, wanted for murder! Look, man, look—that's a serious charge—men have been hung for murder! I don't want no jokin'.'

'We ain't jokin',' the deputy assured him.

'Who am I supposed to have killed?'

'Martin Jones,' the deputy replied.

Martin Jones was a cowpuncher who worked for Big Jim Wilford's huge Triangle Diamond cow outfit, the one big spread in the northern Montana area. Ed Cotton's anger gave way to quick alarm. His mind went back two days. He had been playing poker in the El Dorado and Martin Jones had been in the game. Ed had caught him deliberately cheating—dealing from the bottom side of the deck. And he had called the tough cowpuncher's hand. He had called him a cheat and a skunk.

He and Martin Jones had fought. Ed had finally whipped the cowpuncher, but he had had a tough chore. His lips were swollen now, and he had an eye that was slightly black. But he had knocked Jones off his feet. Jones had

5

fallen to the sawdust floor. He had reached for his gun. But Ed Cotton had moved in quickly and had kicked the .45 from the cowpuncher's grip. His boot had sent the big pistol sliding across the floor to bury itself into the dark sawdust.

Martin Jones had spat blood. His voice had been low and deadly. 'I'll kill you for this, Cotton!'

'Not if I kill you first!'

And now, according to this pair, Jones was dead—murdered—and the words he had uttered in excitement and unthinkingly had come home to brand him a murderer. Ed felt a touch of wild alarm. He looked up at Deputy Sheriff Rome and said, 'I never killed Jones.'

Rome's shoulders moved under his heavy sheepskin coat. 'You can tell that to the justice of the peace, Cotton. But a trapper found a dead man this mornin' along your south fence. This man had cut the wires on your fence, and his fence pliers laid beside him. And that man was Martin Jones.'

Ed frowned. 'Along my south fence—he was cuttin' wires?'

The deputy watched him with cat-suspicious eyes. 'Looked to us like Jones had been headin' for the Triangle Diamond. To keep from ridin' all around your fence, he must've got off his hoss an' cut the wires to take a short-cut. You saw him do this, an' you

6

shot an' killed him.'

'I never killed him.'

The deputy spat tobacco juice on the clean white snow. 'We're all rememberin' the fight you two had in the El Dorado, an' how you each said you'd kill the other. Well, I'm packin' a warrant for your arrest, Cotton.'

'Who filed the warrant?'

'Big Jim Wilford.'

Ed realized this was only logical. Martin Jones had worked for Big Jim Wilford. Also, Big Jim did not like the fact that he, Ed Cotton, had strung wire across range he claimed, even though Ed had done this legally. Ed had filed on a section of government land—six hundred and forty acres. Under federal law he was eligible to file on a homestead, which was a hundred and sixty acres—an area a half-mile square. Because he had recently returned from the Spanish-American war, where he had ridden with Teddy Roosevelt's Rough Riders, he was entitled to another four hundred and eighty acres—a grazing claim—and in fencing this land he had run a fence across Black Canyon, which had springs that ran water all the year round.

The loss of Black Canyon had hit Big Jim Wilford hard, Ed knew. The cowman depended very much upon the water in the deep canyon to keep his herds during the dry spells. Ed Cotton had fenced the canyon with

7

difficulty. He had run wires down the steep slopes, sometimes blasting holes in boulders to insert his fence posts. But he had put the area under wire at long last. Ed had moved into this country looking for peace, and now he had anything but peace. Trouble was staring him in the face.

'Why didn't Sheriff Spears serve the warrant?' he asked.

'You're full of questions today,' grumbled Deputy Rome. 'Spears is out of town for a spell an' I'm runnin' his office. Ed, we're gonna tie your hands an' take you into town.'

'You don't need to tie my hands. I'll go of my own accord.'

But the burly deputy shook his head. His next words were addressed to Cart Nagle. 'Nagle, get that spot-cord rope out from under your sheepskin. Get down an' tie his hands behind him and hang on to the end of the rope so he can't run away from us. I'll hol' my gun on him.'

Nagle showed a thin smile. 'I can handle him, Rome,' he said. He went out of his saddle with the thin spot-cord rope in his hand. 'Turn aroun' so I can tie your hands behind you, Cotton!'

Ed's temper had reached the boiling point. They were not even extending him enough consideration to let him go to town peacefully with them. The weight of his gun under his sheepskin coat was heavy and reassuring. The

8

gambler came closer, rope in hand. Ed knew that he was taking a chance—a deadly and terrible chance of getting shot. But he had to do something.

He hit Cart Nagle in the face.

The blow was not sharp, because Ed wore a mitten. Rather it was a clumsy mauling gesture that lacked sharpness but was not lacking in power. Nagle flung up an arm, but Ed Cotton's fist went over it and he felt his mitten hit the gambler in the nose. Blood spurted instantly. Nagle went backward a pace, and Ed moved in and clinched with him. He wrapped both arms around the slender gambler. He held him this way, and he butted Nagle in the face with his head. He used some of the rough tactics he had been taught in the army. He felt something warm on his face; that would be Nagle's blood. Nagle tried to escape from his grip but could not. He tried to pound Ed in the belly but Ed held the man's arms to his side. Ed butted like a billy goat.

Dimly he realized that Rome had dismounted. Rome had his .45 out and was circling, trying to get in to slug him. But Ed kept Nagle between himself and the angry deputy. Whenever Rome circled, Ed turned the gambler. Nagle was hollering for help, and his screams were broken intermittently by Ed's butting head. Nagle was almost out on his feet.

'Don't shoot, Rome! Don't shoot! You'll kill me!'

'I'll slug—the devil—'

Ed grinned and realized his temper had again got him into trouble. He butted Nagle in the jaw—a solid, jarring blow—and Nagle stopped struggling. Ed held him and looked over his shoulder at Rome, and the young cowman-farmer showed a bloody and twisted smile.

'Rome, I got my gun under my coat. I can get it with one hand and drop this tinhorn, and shoot it out with you!'

'You're resistin' arrest.'

Ed panted, 'You're plumb wrong on that point, Rome! I'm not resistin' arrest. I'm against bein' tied an' paraded down Greener's main street. You let me go to town with my hands and feet loose, and I'll go peacefully.'

Rome stood wide-legged, pistol in his hand. His face was puzzled, and Ed thought he read fear there too. There was a rumour on this range that Ed Cotton was a heller with a six-shooter. Ed hoped the deputy sheriff would take him up on his proposition. He did not want to have to shoot it out with him. He was in enough trouble as it was, with a murder charge over his head.

Rome said, 'All right, you win. Cotton, promise you'll go to Greener peacefully, and we won't tie you.'

'Good.'

'Then let go of Nagle, huh?'

Nagle panted, 'Let me go, Cotton. He'll live up to his word.'

But Ed did not release the gambler. A sudden stab of fear had pierced him. Rome might by lying. He might release Nagle, and then Rome might fire and kill him. This deduction was based on two things: Rome, he knew, hated him; also, Rome could kill him, and he and Nagle could claim the killing had occurred while he had been resisting arrest, and nobody would be the wiser.

His temper had really put him behind the eight ball!

But he had to take the chance. He couldn't hold Nagle all day. The man was getting over his beating, and he was getting ready to fight again. Ed thought, I have to let him go, and go for my gun. But I haven't got a chance—not when Rome has his gun out an' on me—

'What's goin' on here, men?'

Ed realized, with a start, that a man spoke from behind them. Still holding Cart Nagle, he looked at the newcomer. During the fracas, this man had ridden out of the hills, and none of them had heard his coming. Snow had muffled the sounds of his bronc's hoofs. Now he sat his saddle and watched them. He rode a blood bay gelding—a hot-blooded horse that had stockings on his four legs, the white stockings glistening from

11

being washed by the snow. The rider was a wide-shouldered man about sixty years of age. He had a wide weather-beaten face and dull blue eyes.

Big Jim Wilford!

Ed Cotton had never been as glad to see anybody as he was to see the big cowman. Although he and Big Jim did not see eye to eye, he was sure the cowman had saved his life. He released Cart Nagle. The gambler stumbled and sat down in the snow. He was moaning and his face was bloody. He moaned like a whipped puppy. He scooped snow in his hands and started to rub it gingerly on his bloody nose.

Big Jim Wilford asked again, 'What's goin' on here, Rome?'

The arrogance had left the deputy. He was confronting one of the big men of this county—one of the men who ran the area. A note of humility entered his voice.

'You filed a murder warrant on this farmer, Big Jim. Me an' Nagle rode out to serve it. He resisted us an' got his arms around' Nagle an' butted his nose flat with his head.'

Big Jim's glance moved over and settled on Ed Cotton, who was puffing like a wind-broken saddle-horse.

'That right, Cotton?'

Big Jim Wilford's voice had a paternal tone. He sounded like a weary father who had just separated two of his sons who had been

12

fighting.

'To a degree.' Ed breathed easier now. 'I would have gone peaceful if they hadn't pressed me.'

'What did they want to do to you?'

'Tie my hands behin' me. Ride down Greener's main street with me ridin' ahead of them, hands behind me an' one of them holdin' the free end of thet spot-cord rope there.'

'Murder is a serious charge.'

Ed wiped his nose with his coat sleeve. 'I know that Big Jim. I never killed Martin Jones. Me an' him had a fist-fight, yes—we threw hot words back and forth—but that was only our tempers, and not hate.'

Big Jim Wilford looked at Cart Nagle. The gambler was scooping up more snow to hold against his face. But his words were addressed to Deputy Sheriff Fred Rome.

'How come Nagle here rode out with you, Rome? He ain't no lawman.'

'He is now. I deputized him to ride along an' help me.'

Big Jim Wilford allowed a smile to touch his cold lips. 'You ain't much of a hand to pick out a man to side you,' he said. He looked back at Ed Cotton. 'Ed, I'll ride along an' guarantee you you'll get into town okay. An' your hands won't be tied behin' you, either, if you give me your word you'll try nothing funny.'

'You got my word,' Ed said.

The cowman nodded. 'Good enough for me,' he said.

Deputy Fred Rome grunted something and stuck his gun, barrel down, into his overcoat pocket.

The deputy got on his horse. Nagle looked up, and his face was red and swollen. 'Help me on my horse, somebody?'

Ed Cotton laughed dryly. 'You got off your horse by yourself! You're a big boy now, tinhorn, so climb back on all by yourself!'

Nagle gave him a look that was heavy with hate. He staggered to his horse, found his stirrup, and mounted with difficulty.

Big Jim Wilford spoke to Deputy Sheriff Rome. 'Take Cotton's team over to his barn, an' unhook them an' saddle his horse for him.'

Rome said, 'Okay,' but the words came grudgingly.

Ed said, 'My roan is tied to the manger. Saddle him an' turn the work horses loose. Throw the harnesses over the wagon.'

Rome's face was flushed. He rode over and got one of the horses by the bridle and led him and his team-mate to the barn, the barbed wire getting tangled behind the wagon. When he reached the barn he got out of the saddle and started to unhook and unharness the team.

Nagle sat his saddle and said nothing.

'I never killed Martin Jones,' Ed repeated.

Big Jim Wilford said, 'Jones is dead as a man will ever be, Cotton. A trapper come to me an' tol' me about findin' Jones' corpse. I rode over right away to where he had been cuttin' your fence. I never ordered no man of mine to cut your wires, Cotton. But there was Jones, plumb shot through an' dead.'

'A trapper found him, you say?'

'Yeah, thet trapper what traps across the ridge from Black Canyon. Trappin' coyotes over in thet area, I reckon.'

'I don't think I know him,' Ed said. 'But I sure wanta thank you again for hornin' in, Big Jim.'

'Two against one ain't fair play in Big Jim's book,' the cowman said.

Ed asked other questions. The body had been discovered about two hours ago and was now in Greener in the morgue. Big Jim had the body taken to town. He had found tracks where the ambusher had hidden in the brush. 'An' the overshoes he wore was just about the size of your feet, farmer.'

'That's no evidence,' Ed reminded him.

Big Jim Wilford admitted this fact. 'But the fight you an' him had in the saloon—and the words you had between you—they'll count strong against you.'

'I never killed him, like I said. Somebody is jobbin' me, and it might be you. I took up this section of land in the middle of your best

15

range, and I fenced barbed wire acrost Black Canyon, cuttin' you off from your best water.'

'You accusin' me of murderin' my own men?'

Big Jim had a small smile, but his eyes were angry. And he clipped his words.

'No, I ain't, Big Jim. I think you're fair and square. But somebody killed Jones. I don't know who it was—but I know why. Somebody is after me because I run this fence out, and somebody wants me behin' bars for good. So they jobbed me, and Jones got his light snuffed out.'

'That don't make good sense, Ed.'

'I know it don't, but it's true.'

'Well, tell it to the J.P.'

Rome had turned loose the workhorses and they were drifting across the hill, where they would find grass among the boulders where the wind had swept the snow away. The deputy went into the barn and soon came out with the roan, saddled and bridled. Then he mounted and led the horse to where the trio waited.

'Here's your ol' plug, farmer.'

Big Jim rode close to Ed after he had mounted. 'You got a gun on you, Cotton?'

'Under my sheepskin coat.'

Big Jim reached in and got the .45. 'I'll take care of this.' He jammed it in his coat pocket. 'Time we got movin'.'

16

Nagle rode in the lead. His face was blue and swollen and hate welled in his heart. Behind him came Ed, who rode abreast with Deputy Sheriff Fred Rome. And behind Ed and the lawman rode Big Jim Wilford.

The wind was ice cold. Their horses' hoofs made crunchy sounds on the snow. Ed glanced back at his homestead. He had two cows to milk, hogs to feed, and some chickens in the hen house.

'I'll send somebody over to do your chores,' Big Jim said.

Ed grinned but said nothing. For a man who wanted him behind bars, Big Jim Wilford was a very helpful neighbour. Then the thought came that maybe Big Jim was not behind this.

Then who was?

CHAPTER TWO

When the four of them rode down Greener's snow-packed main drag, people stood in windows and on the sidewalks and watched them, and Ed Cotton got the impression that he was a dangerous man being displayed to the citizens. He had a grim smile but his heart was heavy. The courthouse was a log building at the far end of the street, Montana Avenue. They dismounted at the tie-rail, and Ed

17

walked ahead into the office of the Justice of the Peace, with the others following him. The pot-bellied heater was full of lignite and the office was warm. The J.P. was waiting, all importance. The last arrest for murder had been some years ago, and he was an important old man on this windy, snowy day.

Although Ed Cotton had not been on this range very long—only a few months, in fact—he had learned much by keeping his ears pinned back and his mouth closed. He had learned that the old judge had once been a cowpuncher and he had worked almost all his days for the Triangle Diamond outfit, trailing in when the spread had taken its trail herds into this area up the Powder River trail from Texas.

Before working for Big Jim Wilford, the old man had worked for Big Jim's father, down in Texas. But he had become too old and crippled to ride long circles, so Big Jim had pensioned him off. He had come to town and had taken to drinking and gambling. Big Jim's pension had not gone very far. Therefore Big Jim, who was a county commissioner, had had him appointed Justice of the Peace, thereby getting him off his hands and on to the hands of the taxpayers.

'Deputy Rome, you have the prisoner?'

'Here he is, Your Honour.'

The old man liked to be called Your Honour. He studied Ed over the spectacles

18

perched on his wide nose. He looked down at the papers on his desk. Ed wondered ironically if the old buzzard could really read or if he was just putting on an act. This amusing thought must have shown in his face for the J.P. said suddenly, 'This ain't no laughin' matter, Cotton.'

'Yes.'

'Yes, *what*?'

'Your Honour. Yes, Your Honour.'

'Better, Cotton, better. Have respect for your elders and a court of law. You are charged with the heinous crime of murder against the person of one Martin Jones. Do you plead guilty or not guilty?'

'Not guilty, Your Honour.'

The old man cleared his throat noisily. He had a Sioux war hatchet, and he pounded it against the desk, the stone making a ringing noise.

'The jedge of the circuit court won't git here until about March, I understand. Therefore there is only one thing for me to do an' thet is set the amount of your bail. I've already done looked it up in the Statutes of the State of Montany.'

He let the silence grow. Deputy Rome shifted, his overshoes making sloppy sounds because of the snow on them. Gambler Nagle said nothing, gingerly rubbing his jaw. Big Jim Wilford had moved over and now sat on a bench beside the stove.

'Your bail, prisoner, is set at twenty-five thousand dollars.'

Ed Cotton thought, Might just as well be twenty-five million. I haven't got over a hundred bucks to my name.

'I cannot raise that much bail, Your Honour.'

'Then, accordin' to the Law, I have to send you to jail to await trial. Deputy Rome, take the prisoner to his cell.'

'This way,' the deputy said.

He and Ed walked down the short cell corridor, and he put Ed in one of the two cells, then shut the door and shook it a few times to make sure it was locked. Ed walked over and sat on the bunk and watched the deputy return to the J.P.'s office, shutting the door behind him.

Ed Cotton was alone.

The steel bunk hung from the ceiling by two chains and was bolted on one side to the concrete wall. The cell had one window, which was barred and high in the wall. He gave his surroundings a glance and then returned to his thoughts. Fate sure had a way of bucking a man off into the mud, he reasoned.

Somebody wanted him off this range. But who was that somebody?

All the signs pointed toward one man.

And that man was Big Jim Wilford.

But why would Big Jim want him off this

range? Because he had taken up a homestead on Triangle Diamond grass? That was the only logical answer. He had been the first homesteader in this area. If the Triangle Diamond allowed him to stay, then other homesteaders would come in, and barbed wire would completely ruin Big Jim's range, just as barbed wire had ruined the Red River range down in Ed's home state of Texas.

Ed's father had been a big Lone Star cowman, running thousands and thousands of head of longhorn Texas cattle in the Red River country. Then the farmers had come in, and his father had watched his range shrink to almost nothing, and he had had to sell almost all his cattle. Ed had seen the war coming and he had joined the cavalry, first breaking broncs for Uncle Sam's army in Winnemucca at the relay station, over in Nevada. And his boyhood friend, Booger Sam, the Negro, had joined the army with him.

Ed's mother had died in childbirth, and Booger Sam's black mother had raised him and her own son. Ed could never remember a time when Booger Sam had not been with him; he and the coloured man had fought together shoulder by shoulder all the way. The war over, both had been discharged in Georgia; Booger Sam had gone into Louisiana to visit relatives, and Ed had headed north into Montana. During the war, his father had

21

died; the lawyer had sold the remnants of the once proud Texas outfit, and Ed had not even returned to the Red River. Booger Sam should be along any day now. Ed had written to him and had told him the location of their farm.

Ed thought, Lord, I'd like to see that big wide black face, and was achingly lonesome for his big friend.

Booger Sam sure would be surprised to find his partner behind bars.

Ed thought, I have to get out of here.

He could do nothing from inside the bars. But twenty-five thousand—well, it might as well have been millions and millions. Ed lay on his bunk and laced his hands behind his head and did some thinking. But his thoughts got nowhere. They seemed to be running around and around in a circle. The short day ran its course, and when evening came the old jailer came in and lit the kerosene lamp that hung from the wall in the bullpen. It made a flickering yellow light because of the soot-streaked chimney.

'You want some chuck, prisoner?'

Ed sat on his bunk and grinned. 'Only free meal I'll get since the army done discharged me. Sure, I want some chuck, you ol' bandy-legged runt.'

The old man grunted and grinned too. He was about seventy, and as bowlegged as a man could be. He also had spent his life with his legs curled around the barrel of a horse. He wore a big Colt .45 that sagged low on his hip. With his long handlebar moustaches, he presented a woebegone appearance, but Ed Cotton figured the old boy was no easy mark. He could take care of himself in a tussle, Ed knew.

'I'll get you some ham an' eggs from the restaurant,' the old man said, and left. His worn boot heels made loud noises on the concrete. When he came back he had a plate with four fried eggs and three thick slices of home-cured ham. Ed discovered he was voraciously hungry.

The jailer lifted the trap door in the bottom of the cell door and slid through the plate.

'They's coffee in thet can next to the aigs,' he said, and stepped back. 'Eat an' be merry, for tomorrow we die.'

Ed grimaced. 'Lovely thought.

'But the truth,' the old man said. 'And remember I said *we*, not *you*.'

Ed ate and enjoyed the meal. The old man came back after the tray, and Ed shoved it back through the trap door and sat down again on his bunk. Within a few minutes, he had his first visitor. He was very surprised, and he hoped this did not show in his face, for his visitor was Connie Wilford, Big Jim's daughter. She wore overshoes and a long fur coat that failed to hide her feminine charms. The jailer accompanied her back to the cell.

23

'You got ten minutes, Connie,' he said.

'I got the rest of my life if I want to stay here,' she snapped back. 'Get back to your easy chair and your solitaire game and let me talk to Ed alone.'

'Accordin' to regulations—'

'Get movin'!'

Her throaty voice held a joking note, but under it Ed detected sternness.

The jailer grinned and returned to the office. Connie Wilford looked at Ed Cotton. The lamplight showed on her full face with its stubby nose and brown eyes. Ed was still surprised. He had danced with Connie at a couple of the local Saturday night dances, and they had got along amazingly well. He especially liked her free and easy manner; although she broke her own saddle-horse she was still very womanly and pretty in a party dress.

'I'm sorry, Ed,' she said.

Ed grinned. 'I'm even sorry for myself Miss Connie. Now with you sympathizin' with me, I feel a little better.'

'There's a lot about this I don't understand.'

'The same holds true for me, Miss Connie.'

He liked to talk with her. He told her the truth and only the truth, and as he explained her frown became deeper.

'I wonder if Big Jim is behind this?' she said quietly.

24

Ed shrugged. 'Only way I can look at it,' he had to admit. He hastened to add, 'I've thought and I've thought, and it looks to me like Black Canyon and barbed wire are at the bottom of it. Then again, I can't imagine your dad doing such a low-down thing.'

She was frank and honest. 'I don't like to think that either, Ed. But signs point toward him. If it isn't my dad, then who is behind it?'

'You got me up a stump.'

'This puzzles me,' she said. 'But you can do nothing about solving it in jail, Ed.'

'Well do I know that. But twenty-five thousand—' He shrugged and walked back to his bunk and rolled a brown paper cigarette. 'I've never had twenty-five thousand in my life. I never expect to have that much. And my homestead—shucks, it ain't worth but a thousand or so, if anybody would even advance that on it.'

'I've talked to Big Jim about pulling back his warrant. But he claims he won't. When the Old Man gets his mind made up, he's stubborn as a mad bull. Martin Jones was a good hand, and he's been on our payroll for years now, and Dad will go to the hot place for a man of his.'

'I didn't murder him,' Ed repeated.

He was getting tired of repeating that fact, but there seemed nothing else to do but keep on repeating it. He felt the sudden push of raw impatience.

'I believe you, Ed.'

'I'm glad somebody does.'

She pursed her lips. 'I'll talk to the county attorney. He might reduce that bail; it seems terribly large to me. Then I might be able to go your bond, if the bail is reduced.'

'No you don't.'

'I have about five hundred head of cattle, all in my name. I feel sure you never killed Jones. He was shot from ambush. I don't think you're the type that would kill from the brush.'

'But you are *not* going my bail, savvy?'

'Oh, you and your stiff-necked pride! You're as bad as Big Jim!' Anger lighted her pretty face. 'What do you intend to do—sit in this cell and die of old age and anger?'

'They'll be ready to go on with my trial in a month or so. Then I still think the coroner's inquest might bring out somethin'. I'd like to talk to that trapper that found Jones' body. I'll wait for the inquest.'

'That might not bring out a thing. In fact, it might make your case worse. But I am sure willing to see if I can get the bail reduced and if I can go your bond. I'm puzzled about this whole thing, so just lay it all on the threshold of something called curiosity.'

'All right, say you go my bail. Then what will happen between you and Big Jim?' He answered the question himself. 'He'd boot you out of your happy home, girl. No, no, no! I'm not comin' between you an' your father.' He hesitated, groping for words. 'To you I should be just a wayward Texican who has traded his saddle for a plough handle. I thank you, Miss Connie, but I'll never agree.'

'You're more bullheaded than Big Jim. Well, if you change your mind, you know how to get in touch with me.'

'Thanks a million, but I can't do it.'

Her face was red with anger. 'Maybe even if you change your mind—!' She turned and walked away. Hanging on to the bars, still mystified by her offer, Ed Cotton watched her until she went into the office, slamming the door behind her.

The wind was rising. He could hear it howling againt the outside wall. He glanced up at the window, but darkness was on the rangelands. He could see fresh snow piled up on the window sill, though. Winter was here to stay, evidently. He thought of his farm. There were his cows to milk, his chickens to feed, his dog and cat to be fed. With supreme difficulty he controlled his raw impatience. Within a few minutes, he had another visitor. He was as surprised to see this person as he had been to see Connie Wilford walk down the cell corridor.

But this visitor was a man.

He did not wear a rough sheepskin or buffalo-hide overcoat. His overcoat was made of imported wool. He did not wear overshoes. He wore calfskin oxfords and rubbers. His gloves were of fine calfskin, too. He was a wide-shouldered man with a heavy face, cleanshaven and blue in the lamplight. He was the owner of the El Dorado Saloon, and his name was Walt Downing. He had been in Greener town about a year or so, Ed had heard, and he had made money in his saloon and gambling den. Now he smiled and took off his right glove and dug in his overcoat pocket and took out a cigar which he handed to Ed Cotton.

'Sit down, Cotton, and have a smoke with me?'

Ed took the cigar. It was a finely turned Havana Special. He lit it and inhaled its sweet aroma and hoped his face, once again, did not show his surprise. Things had piled up in the last few hours.

'What's on your mind, Downing?'

The saloon owner waved his cigar. 'Don't rush me, Cotton. I been out of town all day and just returned. I heard about your trouble so came over to see you. I hear they want twenty-five thousand to bail you out. That is too much bail. I'm trying to get it dropped to about ten thousand.'

Again, surprise.

'Why worry about me, Downing?'

The cigar was returned to its owner's thick lips. Downing smiled, and his eyes glistened

28

in the lamplight.

'I'll lay my cards on the table. This is strictly between me and you. I don't like Big Jim Wilford and he don't like me. He used to run Greener lock, stock and barrel until I come into town. He doesn't like my saloon and he doesn't like me. I think he jobbed you.'

Ed Cotton decided to play his cards close to his chest and not to tip his hand.

'You want me out of jail to take a slap at Big Jim, eh?'

'That's about it. Between me an' Big Jim, it's a fight to the finish. He's said some wicked things about me. Not to my face, either. I'd like to show him he isn't the big kingpin on Greener range.'

Ed wondered if this were true. He realized it might be laying it on the fact that hate was a rough taskmaster, and a man would do anything in the name of hate. That is, some men . . .

Suspicion rimmed Ed Cotton's words. 'This sounds good, but I smell somethin' more under it, Downing. I beat the stuffin' out of your gambler, Cart Nagle. And you still offer to raise my bail if it is cut down low enough?'

'Nagle only gambles for me. Sometimes he tends bar. He's a hired hand—hired help—and nothing more. He had no reason to ride with that deputy sheriff. But that is

29

neither here nor there. When you fenced Black Canyon you fenced in some of Big Jim's best waterholes—water he'll need bad next fall if the rain is short.'

Ed Cotton listened with half an ear. Although Big Jim was a puzzle to him, so was this saloon man. Downing had other interests, he had heard, besides the El Dorado. He owned part of the bank and the general store. He also was a great hand at gambling. He grubstaked trappers and miners. Ed had also heard that he hired trappers to run out traplines and trap beaver and muskrat along the river and the creeks. Downing always had money—lots of money. He spent it freely, too. The trapper who had found Martin Jones' body had been a man hired by Downing.

'So you want to use my case to get back at Big Jim, is that it?'

'That is it entirely. No friendship involved between you and me, for personally I think anybody who would work with his hands for his bread is a little bit stupid. That's my hand. Take it or leave it.'

'I leave it.'

The man smiled and shrugged. 'Think it over, Cotton.' He turned and went down the corridor and entered the office, and Ed Cotton was alone again. Ed dropped full length on the bunk and wondered if he should not have taken the saloon man's offer.

He could do nothing while in jail. Once on the outside, he could work on his case, and he might find out who had framed him. The hangman's noose awaited him. Then he realized his pride had kept him from accepting Walt Downing's offer, just as his pride had moved in between himself and pretty Connie Wilford.

But there were different motivations behind their offers to get him out of jail. Connie wanted to go his bail because she felt sorry for him. Walt Downing wanted to free him just to take a slap at Big Jim.

His stream of thought was broken by the old jailer coming back with a coal hod and a poker to put more life into the pot-bellied stove. The old man shook down the grates and peered into the box and mumbled, 'This danged lignite coal sure makes lotsa clinkers,' and carried the ashbox out the back door. When he came back he had a rim of snow on his shirt and he was shivering. 'Gonna be a col' night, prisoner.'

Ed had allowed his thoughts to return to Walt Downing. Some claimed that Downing's trappers poached beavers on public domain. Beavers were protected by law, and a man had to get a permit to trap them, and this permit covered only a few pelts. Beaver pelts were worth much money on the market. Their fur was used in the manufacture of hats and in furs for women.

31

Some people had hinted that maybe Downing was also engaged in rustling cattle. Big Jim Wilford's Triangle Diamond cattle, maybe?

'Gonna be a col', col', night, Cotton,' the jailer repeated.

'Keep a good fire,' Ed said, 'or I'll complain to the sheriff.'

'Complain and be darned,' the old man snarled.

Ed grinned and made no reply.

During the night the storm broke with real fury. Wind howled and snow piled up against buildings. Ed was glad he had plenty of thick Hudson Bay blankets. He also had a heavy buffalo robe. The old jailer slept in the cot at the end of the bull pen. He awakened occasionally to stoke the belly of the heater. Ed had no company the next day. He half-expected that Connie Wilford would return; but the girl did not come to see him. Nor did Walt Downing. The old jailer kept Ed informed. Downing and the girl had appealed to the justice of the peace to lower the bail, but the old broken-down cowpuncher would not do this—he was loyal to Big Jim Wilford. The day was cold, and as miserable and as grey as Ed Cotton's thoughts. The next night was also a cold one; so was the following day. Ed was becoming very impatient. The injustice of this was slowly building up into a strong hate. The only trouble was that the hate could not be directed properly because he did not know who had tricked him. On the third night, Ed Cotton broke jail.

CHAPTER THREE

At sundown the wind had stopped for a while, and then had renewed its howling. The thermometer, the old jailer said, was at twenty-three below on the side of the jail, and Ed said it was about that cold inside, too, which made the old man angry and made his poker work angrily among the hot coals in the stove. Ed crawled into bed fully dressed except for his shoes. Sometime around midnight the lash of the storm, howling against the building, awakened him. The fire in the heater had died down. The old jailer lay deep under his sougans and was snoring softly. Ed thought at first that the fury of the storm had awakened him. But this soon proved to be wrong.

What had awakened him had been the sound of a crowbar jimmying the front door. When the door was finally opened, he felt the rush of air even colder than that inside the jail. His first thought was that a lynching bee had been organized to hang him, and then logic told him such an attempt would mean a mob howling and stamping outside.

He could not clearly see the door that led from the bullpen into the office, but he heard boots coming stealthily across the concrete; and soon a big shapeless form was standing in the bullpen.

'Ed? Ed Cotton?'

The voice was low and came from deep in a thick throat. Ed felt a lift of elation, for he recognized the voice immediately.

'Booger Sam!'

The man turned, and now the lamplight showed his face. He was huge, about six four, and his shoulders matched his height. His words had brought the old jailer sitting upright. The jailer wore a red stocking cap to keep his ears warm, and he was garbed in a long flannel nightgown. He looked up into the Negro's face, and his voice was touched with surprise.

'Who are you—how did you get in here—what do you want?'

'The keys to Ed's cell, suh?'

The jailer reached for his gun which lay on the floor. But when he found his holster and gunbelt, the pouch was empty. That was because Booger Sam had stuck the .45 barrel down in his overcoat pocket.

Ed said, 'The keys are hangin' from the hook in the wall over his bed.'

The old jailer had scrambled out of his bunk. He sat on the edge of the bed, and by this time all his sleepiness had vanished.

'Leave them keys be, black man!'

Booger Sam said, 'I reckon I have to git rough with Shorty here,' and he went to work. He twisted the skinny man around, one huge hand on the jailer's mouth, and he laid him on the bed face down. With his free hand he reached up and got the ring of keys. 'Catch, Ed?' he said, and he threw the ring with his free hand, his huge knee on the old jailer's back pushing him into the bedding.

Ed missed the ring, but it landed in front of his cell door. He got down on his knees and reached through; the ring was just beyond his reach.

'Doggone, Ed, never was no good at throwin' anythin'. Kin you make it?'

Ed strained, and his index finger touched the wire loop, pulling it in. Soon he had the cell unlocked and he was out in the bullpen with his old partner and the jailer, who lay and kicked his legs futilely.

'We better tie and gag him,' Ed said.

Booger Sam's white teeth glistened in the dim lamplight. 'Tear up somethin' an' we'll shut off his words with a gag. Little man, quit tryin' to bite the palm of my hand. You ain't a-doin' me no harm.'

Ed went into the office, which also had a light. Booger Sam had bolted the door from inside. Evidently when he jimmied the door the night latch had not been snapped, the regular key lock only locking the door. He had let the night latch snap home. Now nobody could enter from the front door, unless he jimmied the night latch or it were opened from inside. Ed got a length of spot-cord off the hook. He grinned wryly, for it was the same spot-cord that Deputy Sheriff Rome had wanted to tie him with, out there at the farm. He got a towel from the rack—it was black and dirty—and he hurried back to Booger Sam and the jailer.

Within a minute or two, the jailer was bound hand and foot with the spot-cord, and he was gagged with the dirty towel. He lay trussed on the bunk, and the lamplight showed the glistening anger in his old eyes.

'Happy dreams,' Ed told him.

The eyes moved in their sockets. They were marbles being shoved back and forth in the red-rimmed holes. The jaw tried to move, but no words came, for the towel muffled them.

'How we goin' to get out of here, Lieutenant?' Booger Sam asked.

'Out the back door.'

'We got two pistols. I got mine an' the jailer's. But we should have some long guns an' some ca'tridges, and they're both on the rack in the office.'

'We'll get Winchesters,' Ed grunted.

He did not like this idea of a jail delivery. But he knew he could do nothing locked inside the jail. When his escape was discovered, a price would go on his head. The same would hold true for Booger Sam. The jailer would describe the Negro, and although they did not know Booger Sam's name, of course, a price would be posted on his head, dead or alive. There was another disturbing thought, too: because of friendship, Booger Sam had become a hunted man. Because of him, Booger Sam would have a reward on his head. Ed had a moment of despair. It seemed as though of late everything he did or said turned out wrong. But at least he was free to find the killer of Martin Jones.

And that was all that counted.

When they went out the rear door both men carried Winchester .30-30 repeating rifles and had crammed cartridges into their overcoat pockets—shells for their .45 pistols and the rifles. The back door was latched from inside with a staple and hasp, a padlock being run through the staple. One of the keys on the ring opened the lock. They stepped out into a world filled with snow and icy cold.

'This Montany is sure enough cold kentry,' the Negro said huskily. 'I kinda wish I'd done stayed down in Alabamy for the winter.'

'You'd never have seen me again had you done that. By spring my corpse would have been purty rotten in its grave, Booger.'

'I sure did come at the right time, Lieutenant.'

Up ahead of them the back door of a

37

building opened, and Ed Cotton saw a man step into the alley, and then the door went shut behind him. The man was coming toward them but he did not see them, for he had his head down against the push of the wind and snow, and they had pulled back into the doorway of a building.

Booger Sam had a guttural note in his voice. 'Thet man he's coming our way, Looie. Come out of the El Dorado Saloon, 'pears to me.'

Ed said, 'I'm goin' to knock him cold!'

His voice was savage, and this registered on Booger Sam, who sent him a quick glance. Booger Sam did not know that the man was Deputy Sheriff Fred Rome.

'Give him the works, if it pleases your little heart,' the coloured man murmured. 'Ah'll back you up if'n things get tight or somethin' works out wrong.'

'Thanks.'

Head down, the deputy forged ahead. Ed figured he was either going to check the back door of the jail or go to his quarters in the rooming house up the alley. Rome wore a muskrat-skin cap, the flaps tied under his blocky jaw, and he tramped through the snow, his head bent. He did not see the two men there in the doorway of the Mercantile back door. He did not see Ed step forward, rifle barrel raised, nor did he hear Ed come in behind him, for the sound of the wind and the softness of the snow muffled the farmer's overshoes. The next thing Fred Rome knew, the sky had boomed down, and the sky was made of solid rock, and the sky had pushed him down into the snow. He went ahead and landed on his face. He was knocked unconscious.

Ed said, 'Maybe I shouldn't have done it, Booger.'

'He's the deputy what arrested you, ain't he?'

'How did you know?'

'When I come into Greener this afternoon I hung aroun' the saloon, keepin' mah big ears pinned back an' my big mouth closed. I learned a lot. Why shouldn't you have done this to him? He arrested you, remember?'

'He never saw me hit him,' Ed said. 'He won't know now who had the pleasure of knockin' him cold.'

The Negro chuckled deep in his barrel-thick chest. 'Mistuh Ed, you ain't got no imagination at all no longer. Time was in the army when you was full of ideas. This trouble that has done hit you head on has dulled your wits. He'll find out you was delivered from jail. You went out the back door. He got knocked silly in the alley. Add two and two, and what do you git?'

'Five,' Ed joked.

'Let's git movin', Looie.'

'Wonder where my horse is.'

'Your hoss is in the town livery stable, alongside my cayuse. I checked on all thet afore bustin' into thet jail.' The man chuckled as a thought hit him. 'First time I ever broke into a jail, although I onct busted out of one down in Georgia. Them big officials had Booger Sam all lined up fer the chain gang. Ever tell you about thet fracas, Ed?'

'Only about a dozen times.'

They were hurrying down the alley. The livery barn was at the far end of the street. The only light in town, outside of that in the jail and sheriff's office, came from the high rear windows of the El Dorado. Probably an all-night poker game was going on, Ed guessed. They met nobody else on their way to the barn. The barn was open and they had no trouble getting their mounts, for the old hostler was asleep in his room at the far end of the long stable, and he did not awaken. Booger Sam had already saddled the horses. All they had to do was lead them out of the stalls, shove their newly acquired rifles into the saddle holsters, lead the horses out the back door and mount, lifting their bodies against the push of the snow-heavy wind.

Within a minute or two the town of Greener was behind them, hidden in the swirl of the snow. Ed Cotton had a good horse under him, a good rifle in his saddle-boot, and he was armed with cartridges and a short-gun. Beside him rode his old pal from childhood and the army days. And on his head would soon be posted a reward. He was a fugitive from justice.

Booger Sam rode a big roan horse—a horse that had covered lots of miles, but that had been rested by his stay in the livery barn with its good bluejoint hay and oats. Ed Cotton's horse was full of ginger. He pulled on the bit and wanted to run, for he was tired of the inactivity of the last few days when he had been tied in the barnstall, being led out only for water at the town watering trough.

Booger Sam put the roan close, and Ed Cotton could hardly catch his words.

'Done bought me some winter duds when I come acrost Wyomin'. Down in Sheridan, I bought them. Sheepskin overcoat an' a muskrat cap an' overshoes an' California pants—them thick pants. Wonder why they call them California pants when they are made for cold weather. Down in California they tell me it is warm all the year around.'

'A small item,' Ed said.

'What did you say?'

'I said we'd head for my farm first. I wanna see for sure if the chores have been done. Big Jim Wilford promised to send over one of his Triangle Diamond hands to milk my stock an' take care of things.'

'Right nice of him, after it looks like he done railroaded you into the clink, Ed.'

'This has got me puzzled.'

'What did you say? Storm is so bad—'

'We'll get some grub at my place,' Ed said, and grinned.

With their heads down, they rode into the blizzard.

*　　*　　*

The ride to the farmhouse was uneventful except for one incident. They were about two miles out of Greener when suddenly Booger Sam's bronc started to act up. He threw his bony head into the wind and snorted and pranced off the trail, which could barely be seen because of the drift of the snow across it. Booger Sam jerked him around, cursing him for being a bone-headed old fool. Then Ed Cotton's horse engaged in the same antics, and he too pranced and moved to one side, ploughing through the thick snow. Ed curbed him around with savage reins.

'What's wrong with these cayuses, Lieutenant?'

'Mine acts like he smells a wolf.'

'Yep, thet's it. A wolf is out there in the storm.'

But the broncs were not smelling a wolf. They were smelling wild dogs which were in harness. For a dog-sled was drifting through the night, bound for the town of Greener.

'What the heck is thet, Looie?'

Ed peered at the team. From what he could

42

determine, five huskies were hitched Nome style to a low sled. A man was riding the sled, hanging on to the handles. Then they were past them, moving silently into the night. They had come in silence out of nowhere. They returned into silence into the snow-clad nowhere. One moment the dog team and sled were moving past them about a hundred feet away, and then the next moment there was nothing but the storm and the harsh push of the cold wind.

'Dog team and sled,' Ed explained.

'Reckon the driver done seen us?'

Ed shook his head. 'He had his head down in his sheepskin collar. And who would look for two fool cowpunchers to ride out on a night like this?'

'By the same line of reasonin', who would look for a sled pulled by dogs? First time I've ever seen such a thing. They a common thing around here, Ed?'

'They tell me the trappers use dog sleds, an' that is all I know about it. First time I ever seen such an outerfit, too.'

'Drivin' dogs, 'stead of mules or hosses. What a funny country this is, Looie. Reckon dogs can travel over snow faster, though, without boggin' down. What is this I heard tell down in Greener about you fencin' some coulee called Black Canyon?'

Booger Sam rode close to catch every word his partner uttered. Ed told him about his

43

homestead and about fencing Black Canyon and shutting Big Jim Wilford off from some of his best springs.

'So you done blocked him off'n his water durin' a dry spell, huh?'

'Reckon I done more than that, Booger.'

'What you mean by that?'

Ed Cotton explained that to get to the railhead Big Jim Wilford had to drive his cattle down Black Canyon to get them off the mesa. If he did not trek his trail herd down Black Canyon, he had to move his cattle about ten miles to the east, coming off the mesa where it sloped down on to the prairie.

'So you figger he kilt this man Martin Jones to lay the blame on you, so he could git you outa the kentry so he could own Black Canyon again?'

'I doubt that, Booger.'

'On what does you base your doubt?'

'Killin' a man is a serious thing. Big Jim's mad 'cause I beat him to Black Canyon, of course. He never figured a farmer would come into this area, they tell me—figured he was power enough to scare them off even before they settled. But I stole a march on him. He even tried to block my homestead entry and get one for himself on the Canyon, but he couldn't do it.'

'He's got a lot of pull, they tell me.'

'He couldn't do it. My Spanish war record held my claim up, and the government kinda takes care of us veterans, especially so close to the end of the fracas. But he tried.' Ed reined closer so he did not have to shout so loudly. 'I done tol' Big Jim, though, any time he wanted to move cattle through Black Canyon he could do it. So that only leaves the springs he can't use. I aim to use thet water myself.'

'Fer cattle? Thought you was goin' raise head crops an' some root crops, not livestock.'

'That's right. But I aim to run a ditch up to them springs an' run the water down on my property an' use it fer irrigation. They tell me there is only about ten inches or so of rain a year in this area, and irrigation will make any crop grow. Good soil, sandy, with no alkali. This soil can raise anythin' that will grow in this climate, Booger.'

'You don't think Big Jim kilt this Jones fella, then?'

'I doubt it seriously.'

There was a silence. 'Rumour goin' aroun' Greener thet Big Jim's daughter is kinda set on you, Ed. She let it be known she tried to get your bail lowered, but no dice. They done tol' me thet her daddy split his hackamore open when he heard that. You think the female is gone on you?'

'I sure hope so.' Ed grinned in the dark. 'But the thing that gets me puzzled is this: Why would a goodlookin' filly like her want to worry her head about a busted cowpuncher

45

like me, ugly as a mud fence?'

'Cain't never tell about a woman,' the Negro said with the sagacity of his twenty-three years. 'Then if Big Jim never kilt this Jones button, who in Hades did?'

'I don't know, but I aim to find out.'

'How?'

'You got me stumped there, Booger. First, we head for my farm. I want to see if my chores was done.'

'An' pick up some more ammunition an' some grub,' the Negro said.

The little claim-shack suddenly came out of the snowladen wind. Ed opened and closed the barbed wire gate without leaving his mount. His dog was in the house, and he came with a rush in the darkness, barking and almost knocking them down.

'Can we risk lightin' the lamp?' Booger Sam asked.

'I'll light it.'

Soon the kerosene lamp was casting its yellow and flickering glow around the interior of the cabin. The dog, who was not much more than a puppy, made up with Booger Sam, who rolled him on the floor and tussled with him. Ed went first to his barn. His horses were in their stalls and there was hay in the manger. The lantern, lighted in the house, showed they were not tied with halter-ropes; they could wander in and out of the barn of their own free will. His cows had

46

been milked. He had known this before entering the barn, for the milk had been poured into milk pans and had been on the kitchen table, and the dog had had a pan of fresh milk on the floor. He next went to the chicken coop. The hens were on their roosts and the interior of the sod henhouse was warm because somebody had lighted a lantern and had hung it by its bail from a roost-pole. Big Jim had lived up to his word. His chores had been done and had been done right. He did not know that Connie Wilford had done the work.

He returned to the house. Booger Sam had filled the rest of his pockets with short-gun and rifle cartridges. The dog was lying on the bunk, his playful mood gone, watching them with doggish eyes, his long tail occasionally making a half-circle against the bedding.

'Got some grub in thet sack there, Looie. All the canned goods you had on your shelves, which wasn't much.'

'Big Jim Wilford has some line camps out on his range. He keeps them stocked with grub so if a cowpuncher can't make it back to the home ranch in a storm, he has a place to hole up. We can raid his line camps.'

'Then we is ready to drift?'

'Forgot to check on my hogs,' Ed said.

Booger Sam said, 'If the rest of your stock is fed, then your hogs is fed too. Time we drift, man. Thet town prob'ly knows now I

47

busted you outa jail, and blizzard or no blizzard, it's the duty of the law to bring us in.'

'This ain't the first time my fence has been cut in Black Canyon.'

Lamplight glistened on the Negro's dark skin. Lamplight accentuated the white of his eyes and his shiny teeth.

'You don't say!'

Ed told him that the fence had been cut a number of times before. 'But not during the fall. Only after the snow set in an' the weather got cold.'

'Only after the snow came, huh?'

Ed nodded.

'You look aroun' fer tracks, Looie?'

Ed told him he had done that. 'But it got cut each time there was a blizzard. And them blizzards pile up the snow and cover all tracks right pronto.'

'Seems odd to me.'

'Me, too.'

'You don't reckon Big Jim is stealin' cattle south of here an' drivin' them through in a blizzard so he leaves no trail ahind him?'

'I've thought of that, but it ain't logical.'

'On what do you base thet statement?'

Ed pointed out that there was only one other cow outfit between this point and the Missouri River which was about seventy miles to the south. 'An' it is owned by a friend—a life-long friend—of Big Jim's, they tell me.

Man name of Rawhide Nelson. Runs a Runnin' Nine brand, I understand. From what I've managed to learn, Nelson an' Wilford have been friends for years. And who would steal from a friend?'

'Some men would.'

'What we aim to do, Ed?'

'Nothin' much we can do, Booger. Jus' ride the fence and watch it, and catch the gink what cuts it the next time.'

'Another thing we got to do, too!'

Ed studied his partner. 'An' what is that?'

'Keep out of jail!'

CHAPTER FOUR

Connie Wilford had ridden alone to the farm and had done Ed Cotton's chores. Her father had wanted to send a hand over but she had objected, saying it was her job. And her father had looked at her and hidden his wonder. What was his daughter doing—going out of her way to help a stupid farmer?

'Quite a job for a woman, daughter.'

'Don't worry about Connie.'

She had saddled her top horse—a buckskin with a light-coloured mane and tail—and had ridden across the snow-covered hills, heading for the shack of Ed Cotton. The wind was in her face, and she pulled her pretty head down

49

deep between the sheepskin collar of her man's overcoat. The buckskin was grain-fed and grain-hard, and he took the blizzard with long strides. He was a tough horse—a six-year-old. She herself had broken him to saddle when he had been three. They left the road that led to Greener and moved across the hills. Then she was coming down off the foothills toward the cabin which lay below her.

Snow had almost covered the posts on to which Ed had been fastening his barbed wire preparatory to pulling it with his wire stretcher. The wagon was almost covered with snow, as was the small cabin. She went inside, and the dog met her with a lunging burst of affection, and she sat on the floor and rolled him over and played with him for a few minutes, for she liked dogs.

But there was work to be done. First she fed his pigs. Then she milked the cows. She was a good milker. She carried the milk to the house, found a cloth to strain it through, and filled the pans, putting one on the floor for the dog. She did not put it on the softwood floor, but she put it on a rag rug so that if the dog spilled it, it would not stain the clean floor. And the hungry dog started to lap up the warm milk.

She had already fed the cat. The cat had been in the barn watching her milk, and he had had a pan there, and she poured milk into it for him. She lit a lantern and went to the henhouse, the dog at her heels. She pulled hay out of the stack for the cows and the horses. She was a ranch girl, and her practised eye saw that the hay was a mixture of buckbrush and bluejoint, with more of the former. It was not good hay. Another experienced glance at the stack told her that Ed Cotton would be lucky if he had enough hay to pull his stock through the winter.

Ed had done well in the few months he had been on his homestead. He had managed to put up some hay before the winter had come. He had worked hard, she realized. Her mind went to the trouble on this range and the dead man, Martin Jones.

When she had come home after offering to go bail for Ed Cotton—if the bail could be set at a lower sum—she had run into trouble with her father. Big Jim Wilford had been angry and ugly.

'What is this I hear about you offerin' to go this nester's bail if it was set at a lower price?'

'I'm not the only one who tried that. Downing tried to get a lower bail, too, but he didn't come through either.'

'I expected it from Downing. He wants to free Cotton to get him to hit at me, but that bail won't be lowered. I can tell you that for sure.'

Her mother had been cooking at the big wood range. She was a short woman, inclined to be plump, and now she brushed a stray tendril of hair off her sweaty forehead. 'You two quit that eternal fightin',' she said.

'There is something rotten on this range,' her daughter had said emphatically. 'And I think somebody is making a fool out of Dad.'

Big Jim had sent her a long look. 'What do you mean by that, daughter?'

She had explained. He had sworn out a warrant for Ed Cotton. She was sure Ed Cotton had not murdered Martin Jones.

'He called Jones' hand the night before down in the saloon. They both said they'd kill the other. The way I figure, Jones decided to cut Cotton's fence for spite, but Cotton jumped him an' killed him.'

'From ambush?'

'The signs point to it, Connie.'

'All right, they point that way. We'll overlook that angle. But when Rome and that tinhorn gambler come up to arrest Ed Cotton, he's merely trying to untangle some barbed wire. If he was guilty of killing Jones, do you figure he'd be fool enough to stand there and untangle barbed wire, instead of getting out of the country or having a good strong alibi?'

'Cotton is a smart man,' her father had grumbled. 'Sometimes it pays to jes' set tight an' act innocent, 'stead of run.'

'Oh, hogwash!'

Her mother was watching her. So was her father. She felt uncomfortable for a moment, for she knew what the next question would be, and she was correct.

'This Cotton gent,' her father said, 'is jus' a pore misled cowpuncher who has traded his saddle for a walkin' plough. What does he mean to you, honey?'

Connie was an honest girl. 'I like Ed very much. We've danced together and had supper together at a few dances. He's a nice young man. He's ambitious and he's clean-minded and I admit frankly that I like him.' She spoke now to her father alone. 'Dad, I'm sorry you swore out a warrant against him. I think you did wrong.'

'Connie, you seem to forget one thing. A very important thing, too.'

'And what is that?'

'We own the Triangle Diamond cow outfit. It is one of the biggest spreads in Montana. We have a reputation to uphold. This nester moved against us first by fencin' in our water in Black Canyon.'

'He just outguessed you, that's all.'

Big Jim turned a little red.

'So he did. But somebody killed a Triangle Diamond man. Ambushed him and killed him. And somebody has to pay.'

'Even if he is innocent?'

'I don't think this Cotton gent is innocent.'

'You just say that to hear yourself talk!' Now it was Connie's turn to get angry. 'The power of the Triangle Diamond is getting weaker. You're like a dictator. When his empire is threatened, he kills anyone who is his enemy, regardless of whether or not that person has actively moved against him!'

'Daughter, you use rough words!'

Mrs. Wilford had moved in with, 'Both of you—shut up for once. We have enough trouble without your bickerin'!' She'd appealed to her daughter. 'Don't be too rough on Dad. Cattle are at a low price, and this is a rough winter, and our hay is not too good. If you are going over to do Mr. Cotton's chores, then be on your way so you can be back before it is too dark.'

'All right,' Connie said, and went outside.

She had been angry when she had saddled her buckskin. Deputy Sheriff Fred Rome had pressed Big Jim hard to get him to swear out that murder warrant, and she did not like the arrogant deputy. The next morning she returned to the cabin to do the chores, and when she returned home she sewed and did housework and she even made Big Jim his favourite cake—a devil's food. But he grumbled and complained and her mother jumped on him, and she herself was not too happy. The evening before Booger Sam broke Ed Cotton out of the Greener jail, she had met a rider while on her way to do the chores.

She had seen him from a distance—for the storm had momentarily fallen back—and she had recognized his black horse with its blazed face of white. She had waved at him and he had come drifting off the foothills, heading toward her. He had ridden down the slope, his horse sure-footed because of steel caulks, and he had been braced against the work of his saddle, fighting the pull of gravity. His name was Curtis Faver. He was the state game warden and his office was down at the county seat which was Greener. He had a domain to cover that would put a few Eastern states to shame, and his biggest chore was to watch for the illegal trapping of beaver. He was a quiet man, very thin but not too tall. He had a long nose and thin lips, and now his hollowed cheeks were dark with a two-day growth of iron-grey whiskers.

'You'd best head back for Greener, Mr. Faver,' she joked. 'This blow will get harder before the night is over. Dad's got a barometer and the mercury is very low. And besides, there are no trappers out in this direction, are there?'

Faver merely smiled. 'Maybe I'm just out ridin' for my health, Connie. And how is your mother and father?'

'Mother is all right, as usual. Big Jim is a bear with a sore tooth. He's been signing death warrants, the old grizzly.' She was joking, but under her banter was tension. What was this quiet man doing out here miles from his office in this world of endless white snow?

Curt Faver smiled again and shifted his chew of tobacco to the other side of his mouth, putting a bulge in his jaw.

'I done heard about thet trouble with this farmer, Connie. I spent the night at home. Was down south of here along the Big Muddy, checkin' on them beaver colonies down there, and got home last night. Decided to look around this country to check on the trappers scattered here and there. Murder is a serious charge.'

'It isn't good,' Connie said.

'Well, got to drift, honey. Be a good girl.'

'Goodbye, Mr. Faver.'

Connie came to the homestead shack, and mopped the floor to make it as clean as it had been when Ed Cotton had been carted off to jail. She put some coal in the heater and the cooking stove so it would not get too cold for the dog. Maybe she should take the dog to the Triangle Diamond. No, Big Jim would holler—all he did lately was holler—she'd be over in the morning to let the dog out and feed him again

The winter day was short and time was quickly overtaking her, so she worked faster. She was putting hay in the manger of the barn when two men rode into the clearing. They saw her shovelling hay and they rode over to her. Both wore sheepskin coats and overshoes and muskrat caps with the ear flaps tied down. She was surprised to see Deputy

Sheriff Fred Rome riding with the owner of the El Dorado, Walt Downing. And they in turn were surprised to see her.

'Kinda in the wrong place, ain't you?' Walt Downing asked with a smile that she knew was forced.

'Doing Ed Cotton's chores.' She pushed the threetined hayfork into the combination of buckbrush and bluejoint and carried it to the hay window and crammed the hay into the barn. She put the fork in the stack and said, 'That's enough for his stock for the night. He hasn't got much hay left.'

Deputy Sheriff Fred Rome smiled. 'You might have a lifelong chore, Miss Connie, 'cause Cotton might draw life at his trial, or he might even get the noose.'

Connie did not like either of these men. Walt Downing assumed too much importance. Rome, she knew, considered himself quite a lady's man, and he had tried to get every dance with her one Saturday night at the Rock Creek schoolhouse, until Ed Cotton had come to her rescue. Fred Rome had got angry at Ed that night, and all on account of her. What was this pair—this saloonman and this deputy—doing at Ed Cotton's ranch, at this time of the evening and in this snowstorm?

Connie asked, 'How come you two rode all the way out here from Greener in this storm, when you could be sitting close to a hot fire?'

57

She hoped she had made her voice sound casual.

Fred Rome had a ready answer. 'We're jes' ridin' aroun' lookin' over this situation, Miss Connie. Down in the jail Ed Cotton is claimin' up and down that somebody has made it a habit of cuttin' his fence promiscuously. So we decided to do a little investigatin', to see if his word was true.'

Connie looked at Walt Downing.

'We rode the fence from one end to the other,' the owner of the El Dorado said. 'We found it down in only one place, and that is where Martin Jones cut it when Ed shot him from ambush.'

'Cotton is makin' up lies,' the deputy said.

'I offered to go his bail, if I could get it cut down to a sensible figure,' Walt Downing said. 'But I reckon you know that, 'cause you tried the same thing as me. I might offer to go it at twenty-five thousand, if he will promise not to jump the country an' leave me holdin' the sack.'

'He won't run off and jump bail,' she assured him.

'You seem to know him right well,' Deputy Sheriff Rome said.

She felt her anger rise. But she kept her voice level as she mounted her horse. 'Just doing him a favour,' she said. 'Friend of mine . . .'

Walt Downing said, 'He's as bullheaded as

a bull locked in a barn, Miss Connie. Claims up and down he's innocent.'

'He can't prove his innocence in jail,' she said.

Walt Downing asked, 'Then you think he never killed Jones?'

'He didn't kill him. He told me so.'

'Do you believe everything he tells you?' asked Fred Rome. 'When a man's neck is next to goin' into a hangman's noose, he might lie to anybody.'

'I believe him,' she said.

Downing moved in his saddle, stirrup leathers creaking. 'Then if Ed Cotton never shot down Martin Jones, who did kill Jones?'

'I don't know,' she said.

She was glad when they rode away. For some reason she had felt uncomfortable with them around. She finished her chores and rode back to the Triangle Diamond. Her father and she spent the long evening playing cribbage. Usually she was a sharp hand at the game, her keen mind functioning with precision, but on this evening she even mixed up her count, and her father snorted in derision.

'You got eighteen points, woman, and you only took sixteen. Either play right or stop altogether.'

'I'm stopping,' she said, and got out of her chair. She kissed her mother on the forehead. Her mother was sitting in front of the

59

fireplace and was knitting as usual. ''Night, Mother.'

She went to her room and went to bed. Outside, the wind hit the wall and was rebuffed. The stove was warm and the heat was good, but by morning the bedroom would be ice cold. She did not know that her father and mother were talking about her, down in the living room, while Big Jim gathered the pegs and the cards.

'That gal,' said her father, 'is in love.'

'Oh, you imagine things. She just feels sorry for Ed Cotton. What makes you say she's in love with him, Big Jim?'

'She acts about like you did when you fell for me, Mother. Kinda dopey-like, an' your eyes were like hers—they never tracked right.'

'Oh, go on and pick up your cards, and when you say something say something that makes sense. I'm tired of your nonsense.'

Big Jim grinned, but his smile was not happy. Both of his women folks were down on him, and he wished now he had not sworn out the warrant charging Ed Cotton with murder. Then the old stubbornness surged back into him—the stiff-backed stubbornness of the overbearing cattle lord—and he went to his room to escape his wife's tongue. About three in the morning somebody pounded on the front door and Big Jim grudgingly came out of his sleep. He got the lamp lit and

60

sleepily stumbled into the front room and opened the door.

One of his cowpunchers was at the door, covered with snow. Big Jim had sent him to Greener for the mail the evening before and had told him to stay at the hotel and come back in the morning, but here the man had ridden out from town in this blizzard, which did not make sense.

'Thought you aimed to stay in town tonight, Curly.'

Curly came in and shut the door. He stood on the big rag rug so water would not drip off him on to the floor when the snow on his angora chaps melted.

'Ed Cotton done busted out of jail this midnight, Big Jim, so I decided to come out an' tell you.'

'*He what?*'

Curly told about Ed Cotton jumping the Greener jail with the aid of a giant Negro who had come into town, and who evidently was an old friend of the farmer.

By this time, Mrs. Wilford and Connie were in the living room, both wrapped in their warm dressing robes. They were standing in front of the dying fire in the fireplace, and they were listening.

Curly told them that Deputy Sheriff Fred Rome had wanted to organize a posse and attempt to trail the pair, but none of the townsmen would ride with him because of the lateness of the night and the storm.

'Come daylight Rome aims to get his men together, though,' the cowpuncher related. 'But by then the tracks they left will be gone in this blizzard. Wonder if Cotton will jump outa Montany north into Canada?'

'He'll be sensible if he does just that,' Big Jim said.

Connie said, 'He won't run.'

Big Jim was angry. His bony face showed red in the lamplight. 'How come you know so much about this Cotton gent, young lady?' He answered his own question. 'You don't know nothin' about him, woman! You jes' think you do, that's all!'

Curly could see that a fight was brewing and he wanted nothing to do with it. 'Gotta get to the bunkhouse,' he said.

He left, leaving a little pool of water on the rag rug. Big Jim was silent for a moment, the lamplight throwing his bony face into savage relief. This put a new angle on this case. With Ed Cotton free and armed, Ed might pay him a visit. Had he not sworn out the murder warrant? Big Jim did not like this thought. This Ed Cotton was a Texan—he'd fought through the toughest part of the war with Teddy Roosevelt's Rough Riders. At that moment, Big Jim Wilford wished he had taken the advice of his wife and daughter and had not taken out the warrant. But there was no use crying over spilled milk. He turned to look at Connie, but she had left silently. His wife had a mop, and was sponging up the snow water left by Curly. Big Jim almost said something mean to her, for her mania for cleanliness was enough sometimes to drive him wild. But he held his tongue and went to his bedroom, his old moccasins shuffling on the cold floor.

CHAPTER FIVE

Next morning, to escape talking to his wife and daughter, Big Jim Wilford had breakfast with his hands in the mess-shack. After eating, Connie saddled her sorrel and rode to do the chores at Ed Cotton's farm. She knew that from now on she would be a watched woman. Deputy Sheriff Fred Rome would watch her night and day to see if she could not eventually lead him or one of his posse members to Ed Cotton.

She wished that the sheriff had been in his office during this trouble, for the sheriff was an older and wiser head. But he had gone to the state capital for a law officers' meeting, and would not be back for a month or so, she had heard. So Fred Rome was in reality the sheriff—the acting sheriff. The day was clear and cold and there was no wind; the blizzard had blown itself out. She had expected that

Rome had stationed a man to watch the Cotton farm, and she was feeding the hogs a mixture of grain and water when the man came unexpectedly into the hog pen, a grin on his face. His hide was peeling from frost-bite, she saw. She knew him, just as she knew almost all the men on this range.

'Hello, Hank.'

'Busy, Miss Connie?'

'Almost through with my chores,' she said. The hogs were grunting as they pushed at the trough, moving each other to one side. 'You staked out here to look for Ed Cotton if he rode in?'

'So Rome ordered,' Hank Greentree said. 'Was up in the bresh on the side hill when you done rode in.'

'You gonna trail me out of here, to see if Ed makes contact with me?' Derision was in her voice.

He grinned, and she noticed he was toothless. He never had got along very well with those store teeth, his wife had told her and her mother.

'Not my job, Miss Connie,' he said.

'Well, if you're gonna be stationed here, why don't you do the chores?'

'Not my job.'

'The county is paying you good money. You should earn it.'

The smile was even wider. 'You sound like Big Jim Wilford, Miss Connie. He always spouts about bein' a taxpayer an' how inefficient the county is run. Not my job.'

'You don't think for one minute that Ed is so stupid he'd ride into his farm and into your trap, do you?'

The man shrugged. 'Rome's orders. An' Fred Rome is as good as sheriff now. He done hired me, so I takes his orders.'

Connie said nothing. She knew the man was dirt-poor. These few days working for the county would mean much to him financially. He was a rather harmless man, and she wondered what would happen if Ed Cotton did really ride into his homestead and had a clash with this man. This man might fire from the brush, though. She did not like that thought. If Ed communicated with her, she'd tell him his farm was being watched. But he probably knew that already.

She rode back to the Triangle Diamond. Her sorrel was a trail-wise horse, sure of foot because of his steel-shod hoofs, and the wind was not blowing and, without the wind, the day did not seem so cold—although when she had left home the thermometer on the back porch had registered thirty-four below zero. She kept her eyes open but she could not see that anybody followed her. However, all a man had to do was stay with the higher areas and hide in the buckbrush and scrub timber along the ridges, moving through this area of darkness that protruded through the snowdrifts.

She came to the big Triangle Diamond outfit. Snow was piled against the buildings, and snow shovels, handled by disgruntled cowboys, had cleared paths between the buildings. She rode into the barn and dismounted and started to strip her saddle from the sorrel. The barn was the outermost building, and about fifty feet behind it was the base of a hill that was now dark with buckbrush that protruded from the snow. She noticed that the back door of the barn was open and a draught was going through the stall aisle, so she went back to shut the door.

Ed Cotton was standing beside her father's big grey saddle-horse, and she stepped back in surprise.

'Ed!'

'Connie, don't holler or let anybody know I'm here! But I had to see you—I came in the back door—'

She had recovered from her surprise by now. Her mind told him he had used his brains—he had come to see her in the place they would be most unlikely to look for him, her father's ranch. 'I just came back from doing your chores,' she told him. 'Everything is all right at your farm.'

'Booger an' me was there last night, after we busted out of jail. We took all the canned goods off the shelf. I see that guy from town named Hank is watching the spread from the hill.'

'Yes, the place is watched.'

Ed Cotton grinned.

'That means we can't do the chores there, Miss Connie. So if you or one of the Triangle Diamond hands can carry on for me for a few days . . . well, I sure would appreciate it.'

'I'll see your chores are done, Ed.'

Her eyes met his. Then Connie looked away, and she was angry with herself for blushing. With difficulty she found her tongue.

'They'll watch me, too,' she said, 'for Rome will figure we will meet sometime. You did the best thing by riding into the ranch like this—but I think you had better go now, Ed.'

'Maybe I shouldn't have jumped jail,' Ed Cotton said slowly. Plainly he was an extremely puzzled young man. 'But I had to get out. Those bars—they were drivin' me loco. Connie, you don't know what it means to get your freedom taken away from you.'

'You had best go, Ed.'

'Rome is out to get me,' Ed Cotton said, 'and there seems to be more than a murder charge behind it too. But, like you say, I'd best pull out. You want to know what my plans are?'

'No, I don't.'

He frowned. 'I can trust you, Connie, I know that.'

'I still don't care to know your plans.'

'Why not?'

'If I don't know them, then I won't be in danger of revealing them through a word or so that might slip out. It's best you don't tell me, Ed.'

His face was grave. 'Yes, that is right. Goodbye, and thanks a million.'

'Goodbye, Ed.'

Without another word, he left by the back door. She shut the door behind him, sliding it shut on its overhead runners and rollers. The rollers protested in the cold. She did not look out the low window for two reasons. It was so dirty with cobwebs and dirt one could hardly see through it. Also, she knew he would dart behind the haystack and then, from the concealment of the stack, dart into the protective brush. It had been good seeing him again. Her heart was beating exceptionally fast, she realized. Was she in love with Ed Cotton?

Ed reached Booger Sam in safety. The Negro was high on the slope, standing in the windbreak of some huge granite boulders that were almost covered with snow. Booger Sam showed his wide smile as his friend came into view.

'You git to see the woman, Ed?'

Ed told about his talk with Connie.

'You got a good woman thar, Looie.'

Ed smiled. 'I got a good woman? Shucks,

68

she might be doin' my chores jes' out of sympathy, an' fer no other reason.'

'You got her plumb wrong, I thinks.'

Ed decided to change the subject. Connie would keep on doing the chores at his farm, so everything would be all right there. They would stay miles away from the farmhouse, and would just patrol the fence.

'She tol' me about seein' Curt Faver, the game warden, on the range the other day,' Ed Cotton said. 'Wonder what the heck he means by ridin' through this snow, 'stead of stayin' home by the fire?'

'We done seen him, too. From the distance, remember? Anyway, you said it was this game warden gent.'

'He's up to somethin'.'

Booger Sam rubbed a frost-bitten cheekbone. 'Wonder what it is?'

'Don't know.'

'We'd better head back for the high kentry, Looie. From up in the timber, we can watch the kentry below. An' we kin make a fire an' keep warm.'

They rode toward Black Canyon. They came to the beginning of the canyon, which was the north end. The canyon was a natural passage off the bench country to the town of Greener and the lower river country. The bottom was at least a hundred yards wide, even at its narrowest point, and the descent was slow and easy, for the canyon was about four miles long. When the snow finally melted, water would rush down the canyon, and this water, sinking into the sides of the gorge and into the bottom, would replenish the springs the Triangle Diamond had owned, had lost, and so badly needed. They saw a rider once in the snow-filled distance, but he was a Triangle Diamond man pushing toward the home camp, and he rode away until the stillness and the coldness claimed him. There was no sun. There was only the greyness of the snow and the greenness of the fir and pine on the far timbered slopes. They made camp on the side of Echo Mountain, and there in the rocks they built their fire. Ed had shot a jackrabbit, and they broiled his flesh. He was an old jack, and eating his flesh was like chewing springs—your teeth uncoiled and flipped back at you. But he was meat, and a man needed meat in his belly to fight this cold.

'Mebbe we oughta jump outa this section of Montany.' Booger Sam held his thick fingers over the tiny flame. 'This kentry is almighty col' for a boy what was raised in the Deep South. Much colder even than one of them Northerners when they blow up on the Panhandle over around Amarillo an' Lubbock down in Texas.'

'I'm not leavin',' Ed said with deliberate slowness. 'I aim to keep my homestead. I aim to settle down for good and always.'

70

'A bullet or two might settle you down under the sod,' the Negro said. 'Better to be a live coward than a dead hero.'

'Oh, forget it,' Ed said angrily.

They spent the night on Echo Mountain, up high in the boulders. The huge rocks broke the wind and made a rough form of shelter. They had debated about spending the night in a Triangle Diamond line camp but had grudgingly discarded this plan as being too dangerous—both felt sure the line camps might be watched. The night was cold—bitterly cold. Ed Cotton got so cold that he almost consented to jumping out of this section of Montana and coming back to fight when spring came. But this plan was not good, so he discarded it.

He was thankful to be out from behind bars, even if the world were grey and icy-cold. He thought of his cabin. It was *his* cabin—*his* home. His thoughts went to Connie Wilford. She was on his side. No, he would not leave. He would fight until this mystery was solved . . . or he was dead.

There was another angle to consider also. By this time Deputy Rome would have got word to the railhead, down at Sundance, and news of their escape would have already gone up and down the wire, and they might not be able to escape this section, even if they tried. No, the only thing to do was to stay and fight it out!

71

He shivered. He lay in a ball, saddle blanket and another blanket over him. Their horses were on picket-ropes on the slope of the hill where the wind had swept much of the snow away. There they could find a little grass. Not much grass, but they could forage a little, and that counted. Ed slept toward morning, and when he awakened he was wrapped in a cocoon of snow. He struggled out of it and looked at a world that was surly and grey. Beside him about ten feet away was another pile of snow, and he waded over to this and found Booger Sam under it. Soon the Negro was sitting upright, brushing snow from his face and shoulders.

'Another day, Looie.'

'But not another dollar,' Ed said, and grinned.

'How about some chuck?'

Ed was the cook. The cast-iron skillet was the chief implement he used. In it he first made coffee and then heated snow to warm water and made some hotcakes. It was not much of a meal. But it filled the coldness of their bellies momentarily with warmth. Before they had finished eating, the snow started. It came down in giant flakes. There was no wind, and for this both were thankful—wind made the cold seem even more intense. They buried their grub cache under a big boulder, and soon the snow had covered it and hidden it. They marked the location by the tip of the boulder sticking out of the snow and by a scrub ten paces away—the only twisted scrub cedar in this area. Then they were ready to move again.

They rode toward the homestead. Ed and Booger Sam had decided not to ride too close to the barbed wire fence, for it would probably be watched. They reached the high hill north of the homestead shack. Four riders were riding into the yard at this moment, and Ed put the field glasses on them.

'One is Walt Downing. One is Cart Nagle, dang his black soul to perdition.'

'One looks like thet Rome fella,' Booger Sam said. 'Betcha he still has a headache.'

Ed smiled. 'Yep, one is Deputy Fred Rome. And the other—he looks to me like Sheriff Spears. Spears must've come into town ahead of time, or else they got word to him about this trouble an' he come back to take command.'

'What kind of a gink is this Spears?'

Ed said he did not know for sure. Spears had been sheriff for years and years, he understood.

'I've talked to him a few times. This is a big range, but there ain't many people on it, so everybody gets to know everybody else in a hurry. He seemed like a fair enough shooter to me, but a man can never tell by talkin' to a guy once or twice.'

'Or a hundred times,' Booger Sam said.

'What gets me is this: Why does this gambler and that saloon man ride with them?'

'Maybe they got deputized.'

Ed Cotton agreed with this. The wind sighed through the pine and cottonwoods, and the snow fell in slanting sheets, but it was not thick enough to obscure their vision completely.

Booger Sam said thickly, 'Betcha they got bounties out on my head an' on yours too, Ed.' He grinned ruefully. 'Here I thought I'd settle down with my ol' buddy fer the winter an' trap some coyotes an' bobcats an' peddle the hides for my tobaccer money.'

'There'll be money posted on us, no two ways about that. Yonder from the direction of the Triangle Diamond comes a rider.'

It was hard to see through the drifting snowfall. But the rider was a man—evidently a hand Connie had sent over to do the chores. He rode into the yard and dismounted and talked with the four men from Greener, and then he went to the house. Ed's dog came out and romped in the snow, running in a circle around the four Greener men. Ed felt lonesome for his dog. He felt lonesome for his house, too. This renegade life was not too pleasant.

Ed watched the dog plough through the snow. After a while he ran out of wind, and sat beside the house and watched the men. He heard one of his cows bawl, the sound

74

coming up the slope. It too sounded lonesome. Then he thought, My imagination is running away with me. The words of Booger Sam broke into his thoughts.

'Reckon them four come out to your place to check if you had been aroun', Looie,' Sam said. 'They sure don't figger we're dumb enough to stay nights in your cabin, does they?'

'They may think we're that dumb, but I hope we aren't.'

'Let's ride some fence, eh?'

Ed and Booger Sam rode off the slope, keeping the rise of the snow-covered hill between them and the men at the cabin. They found the fence cut in one place. Ed dismounted and looked around, but he could find no tracks. He kicked the snow around and grumbled and wondered why and who had cut the three strands of barbed wire. The newly fallen snow hid all tracks. Had somebody done it just for the heck of it, or had a rig or a man on horseback cut the fence because it blocked his way? Maybe a rider had cut across country and had cut the fence to get through to ride to Greener. He knew that because he was an outlaw now, riders would have no respect for his fence. But the fresh snow had securely and completely covered all tracks.

'Yore fence ever git cut in the summertime?' Booger Sam asked.

75

Ed shook his head. 'Never cut once during the summer, Booger.'

'Wonder why then it gits cut come wintertime an' snow?'

Ed frowned and rubbed his whiskery jaw with his mitten. The sound was harsh in the snowy stillness.

'Was this fence cut yesterday when you come along it?' Booger Sam asked.

'No, it's been cut during the night.'

They patched the fence as best they could, for there was some loose wire hanging from a post—wire Ed Cotton had left there for repair work. The wires sagged, of course, for he had no wire stretcher.

'Why we patchin' it, Ed?'

'Just to see if it is cut again.'

'Me, I sure don't understan' about this.'

'You got company,' Ed commented dryly.

They climbed on their mounts again. Their horses were tired and weary because of much riding and lack of feed. Ed realized they would have to get some feed—grain or hay—for their saddle horses. The only place he figured they could get these essentials was at some Triangle Diamond ranch line camp. They decided to drift north. Ed said there was a line camp back closer to the Canadian Line.

'We ain't gittin' no place, Looie,' complained his big partner. 'Around an' aroun' in a circle we is travellin'.'

Ed nodded. 'We only got one thing to do.'

'An' that?'

'Corner some of these men an' talk to them. I'd sure cotton to lay hands on this Rome or Nagle.'

'Why?'

'Try to make them talk. They're in on this, whatever it is. They showed that when they tried to kill me when they arrested me. If Big Jim hadn't come along, it would of been candles out for this sodbuster.'

'You figger Big Jim might have murdered this Martin Jones feller?'

Ed shook his head. 'I can't imagine Big Jim doin' such a low thing. An' I can't for the life of me find a reason why he would knock down this Jones gent. But a man can never tell.'

'We need grain for our hosses, Looie.'

They rode northward, horses plodding through the loose snow. Snow formed on their sheepskin collars and snow covered the forks of their saddles. Once on the high rimrock, they drew rein to rest their broncs and to look at the territory they had ridden across. The snow had ceased falling and they could see four riders moving along the fence. Rome, Spears, Nagle and Downing. They rode past the repaired section of the fence and did not stop. They were mere pinpoints of dark moving across the expanse of the wilderness, whose whiteness was broken only

77

by bare ledges and trees and black shrubbery. They were evidently heading back toward Greener. Ed and his partner pushed on.

'Ain't so cold today,' Booger Sam said, blowing his breath out suddenly. His breath made a white small cloud.

'Good for us.'

They reached the line camp, and while Booger Sam sat his bronc back on the slope, Ed rode down. Vigilance was in him. They had watched the cabin below for about an hour and had seen no signs of life. No smoke came trickling up from the stovepipe chimney. But that meant nothing. If somebody were at the camp, he might have coal in the stove; coal made little if any smoke. Cottonwood chunks made lots of smoke, and so did scrub cedar firewood. Ed had both mittens off and his rifle in his hands. But his carefulness was wasted, for the cabin was deserted. The door was unlatched and open slightly. Snow had blown in on the floor. Ed found a hundred pounds of oats in a sack leaning in the far corner. Mice had eaten a little of it, and he tied the hole with string he found on the table. He put two cans of pork and beans in his pockets and went to his horse, carrying the oats sack. With difficulty he mounted and rode back to where Booger Sam waited in the brush.

'Our horses eat,' he said.

'Good.' Booger Sam looked at the cans of

pork and beans. 'An' we fills our bellies too.'

They put two mounds of oats on the hardened snow, and the horses started to eat. Booger Sam opened the cans of pork and beans with his jackknife, and they ate the beans without warming them, using their pocket knives for forks. Their horses finished eating and nuzzled the oat sack, wanting more oats. This they did not get.

'We'd better tote those oats with us,' Booger Sam said.

'That's right.'

Booger Sam leaned back against the boulder and sighed. 'Shore wish I had a cigar,' he said. 'One about a foot long. I'd sell my soul for a cigar, Looie.'

'You haven't got a soul,' Ed Cotton joked.

CHAPTER SIX

That afternoon they hunkered in the buckbrush along the top of a hill and watched a man who moved below them. This man was on foot, leading his horse, and he walked across the snow-covered surface of a small creek which was frozen over solid. He paid some attention to a beaver dam that reared its dark surface out of the snow, a conglomeration of sticks, mud, and rocks. The beavers had built the dam and it had stored up quite a bit of water, for the beaver colony was rather large. Had not the beavers built the dam, the creek would have been dry, for water ran in it only after rains or thunderstorms, and then it quickly tumbled down into Black Canyon and roared into the river out of Greener.

'You say thet fella is this game warden, Looie? Fella name of Curt Faver, eh?'

Ed put down his field glasses. The man was about a quarter of a mile away. Plainly he was scouting for the entrances to the beaver dens. He also seemed to be looking for tracks, but these he could not of course find—if there were any to find. For the snow had covered all tracks.

'Wonder what he's doin', Ed?'

Ed put the glasses in the case and buckled down the lid. 'Seems to be lookin' to see if anybody has been trapping beaver. He dug into one entrance to see if a trap was set there. Or so it looked to me.'

'Some of the boys might be trappin' beaver illegally, huh?'

'Could be,' Ed said.

'Looks to me like they is a little water runnin' over that dam, even if the thermometer is this low.'

Ed agreed to this. Because of the speed of the water running over the dam, the water froze only when the thermometer got real low. He knew there were beaver in this creek.

80

He had seen them in the evening when he had ridden range. One night he had left his horse back in the rocks and had gone ahead on foot and had sat on the bank and had watched the beavers at work building their dam. Finally one had caught his scent and had slapped his tail on the water to warn his fellows of the presence of a human. The sound had been as sharp as a rifle report. One moment the creek and banks had been thick with busy beaver; the next, the water was still, the bank deserted. And the beavers had swum underwater to their dens along the bank.

'I don't know much about the habits of a beaver,' Booger Sam informed him. 'But it stands to reason they have two entrances back into their homes in the river bank. One level with the water—an' it freezes solid each winter—an' one below thet top hole, in the water, so they can get home under the ice.'

'That's right.'

'Then to trap a beaver all a man would have to do is cut a hole in the ice an' set his trap an' reach down into the water an' set the trap back in the bottom hole?'

'Right again.'

'Then when the beaver comes out he gets caught. The chain is froze in the ice, an' he fights an' drowns hisself, huh? So the trapper chops the ice open again, takes out his beaver, an' resets the trap?'

Ed merely nodded.

'This Faver fellow must be lookin' for traps. Thet crick is on your land, too, ain't it?'

'It sure is.'

'Then they ain't nobody supposed to trap there except you, an' you're supposed to get a permit to trap, huh?'

'That's the deal.'

'Did you get a permit?'

'No. I tried to get one, too, but Faver turned me down.'

'How come he did thet?'

Ed explained. To get a permit to trap beaver there had to be visible signs that the beaver colony had created havoc in the trees and brush with which they built their dams. But according to Faver this colony had not done enough damage to the surrounding timber—box-elders, cottonwoods, and diamond willows—to warrant being trapped.

'So he wouldn't issue you a permit, Looie?'

'He wouldn't.'

'He must be suspicious thet somebody is trappin' beaver illegally down there. He must be lookin' for their sets. You ain't been poachin' no beaver, has you?'

'No, much as I'd like to, I ain't.'

'Beaver pelts is worth a lot of money now, they tell me. I read a article in a paper about them—use the fur for hats mostly, an' beaver hats cost money.'

'There's money in that crick below,' Ed

had to agree. He had a sudden hunch. 'I'm ridin' down to talk to Faver.'

'What about?'

'Find out what is new.'

'He a friend of yours?'

Ed Cotton swung into saddle. 'With money on his head, no man has a friend. My only friend is you an' my dog.'

'An' mebbe Connie Wilford.'

'Watch my back trail,' Ed said. 'Though I don't look for Faver to raise no trouble. He's a sensible man, an' he has a woman an' children.'

'Then he ain't sensible,' said Booger Sam, and he grinned widely at his own joke.

Ed rode down the slope. Once he glanced back. Booger Sam was in the brush, rifle on Faver, Faver saw him coming, and he stood with his hands held a little way from his sides to show he did not aim to pull his gun. Ed rode up, and he held his right mitten high, holding his reins with his left hand. The oats had put new life in his horse.

Ed said, 'I never come to cause trouble, Faver.'

'I want no trouble with you, either.'

Ed gave the man a glance. Faver's rifle was in the saddle-boot. His short-gun, if he carried one, was strapped under his long sheepskin coat. Ed glanced back up the slope to where Booger Sam crouched with his Winchester. Curt Faver saw the glance and

83

asked, 'Your partner—he's up there on the side hill?'

'With a rifle,' Ed Cotton said.

'I'm a game warden, not a sheriff or a deputy,' Faver carefully pointed out. His sharp blue eyes were quick against Ed Cotton's face. 'You're in a mess of trouble, Cotton.'

'You tell me nothin' I don't already know.'

'There's a thousand bucks on the heads of you two.'

'A thousand for both . . . or a thousand for one?'

'A thousand for each one of you. Two thousand altogether.'

Ed grinned without mirth. 'Makes me feel better. Makes me feel more important.' His eyes flicked along the creek bank and rested momentarily on the sunken recesses of snow that told him where the beaver entrances were located. 'Don't figure nobody is trappin' this crick, Faver. On my property, for one thing, and I have no permit, as you well know.'

'Reckon nobody has traps set here,' Curt Faver said. 'But I just checked to make sure.'

'They tell me there is lots of illegal beaver trappin', seein' pelts are so high.'

Faver had dull eyes that told nothing. 'There might be,' he said slowly. He seemed uninterested, and evidently the topic bored him. But Ed knew this was just a pose. Underneath, the man was as tense as a coiled spring.

'Somebody is cuttin' my fence,' Ed said.

Faver shrugged. 'None of my business,' he replied. 'My job is to ride herd on fur-bearing animals and not a fence, Cotton. Report it to Sheriff Spear.'

Ed smiled. 'You tryin' to be funny?'

Faver had lifeless eyes. 'Not a bit, Cotton. But I'm not after your hide, a thousand bucks or no thousand bucks. I don't know who is cutting your fences, or why they are being cut. In other words, I want no trouble with nobody.'

'Well said,' Ed replied.

Ed Cotton turned his horse and rode back to where Booger Sam waited for him in the brush. He had accomplished nothing by talking to Curt Faver. He had a strong feeling of futility. Everywhere he turned he ran into dead-end trails. The only thing he had learned definitely from the game warden was that he and Booger Sam were worth a thousand dollars apiece, dead or alive. And this knowledge had added not one bit to his pleasure. Nor did it add to the happiness of the Negro, either. Booger Sam grinned and said, 'Never before has I been worth so much, Lieutenant.'

'And maybe never again,' Ed joked rather sickly.

They watched Faver mount and ride toward Greener. Booger Sam wondered if the game warden would report to Sheriff Spears the fact he had been accosted by Ed Cotton. Ed shrugged and said he did not know. Besides, what difference did it make if he reported the meeting to the lawman? He was impatient and he wanted to solve this, and it all went back to the killing of Martin Jones. He decided he would ride to the Triangle Diamond and talk with Big Jim Wilford to try to determine if the cowman were lying or telling the truth about the death of his hired hand. This was a mystery that intrigued him . . . and was heavy with danger.

Booger Sam shook his head dolefully. 'I don't cotton to thet plan, Looie. We might ride smack dab into rifles.'

'We got to take the chance.'

'Wahl . . . all right then.'

They headed across country. The thermometer was falling, Ed figured. They kept to the high ridges for two reasons. One, the snow was not so deep on the ridges, for the wind swept it away. Also, from the high points they could see the rangelands below them. Altitude helped them pick out potential enemies before those enemies spotted them. But they ran into no trouble on the ride to the big Triangle Diamond outfit. They came in behind the big sprawling ranch-house and they watched the place through field glasses. Within ten minutes or so a rider came out of the house and went to the barn and came out

86

riding a bay gelding. He took the trail that led to Greener.

'Looks like thet gambler gent to me,' breathed Booger Sam.

Ed Cotton nodded. 'None other than my bosom friend, Cartwright Nagle. Been visitin' at the Triangle Diamond.'

'Mebbe he has been courtin' Miss Connie.' The Negro sported a tight and amused smile that Ed did not like for some reason, any more than he found himself liking the man's words. But Booger Sam was only joking with him, so he pushed his irritation to one side.

'He's got a big enough name,' Ed joked. 'Cartwright. What a handle, eh? Wonder they didn't name him Egbert.'

'Or mebbe Elmer.'

Ed said, 'Headin' for Greener, he is. That man seems awful interested in two men, one of them named Booger Sam and the other named Ed Cotton.'

'You beat him up. Mebbe he wants revenge.'

Ed said grimly, 'He might have a run-in with me again. I'd cotton to it. You stay in the brush with your rifle. I'll walk in the back door and see what is what.'

'Mebbe Big Jim ain't home.'

'We got to chance that.'

But Big Jim was at home. Ed went in the back door without knocking, and he had his short-gun in his hand. He walked across the kitchen and into the living room where Big Jim Wilford sat in front of the fireplace reading a newspaper. The cowman glared at him over his spectacles.

'What the devil you doin' here, Cotton?'

'I came to talk to you.'

'Then come the way a man comes, not like a criminal! Knock on the door and ask to be admitted and keep your gun in its holster!'

Ed holstered his gun and grinned. 'I never liked and way I entered, either,' he said. 'But there's a thousand bucks on my head . . . an' you put it there, Big Jim Wilford.'

The front door opened and Ed moved back against the wall, hand on his gun. But it was Connie who entered. Her face was rosy from the cold and she looked prettier than ever, her face tucked down in the big collar of her coat. She took off her mittens, her eyes on Ed.

'Never expected to find you here, Ed,' she said. 'Back door man now, huh?'

Ed wondered whether she was angry or if she was joking. Sometimes he did not understand her. He decided she was angry.

'Back door man,' he murmered. 'Made that way by a framed-up murder, and your father signed the complaint.'

She threw her mittens in a chair. 'Been out feeding my chickens,' she explained. She studied him coldly. 'If you want to know, Dad withdrew his complaint. There is no warrant out for you now charging you with murder.'

Ed swung his eyes on Big Jim, who was sucking his pipe with fierce determination. The cowman had no shirt on, and his red braces were bright slashes against his dull grey underwear.

'That true, Big Jim?'

'She doesn't lie.' The cowman's voice was thick. 'The Wilfords never yet have sired a liar to the best of my knowledge. Yes, I withdrew the complaint. The warrant is dead.'

Ed spoke cynically. 'Sure, after it was too late. The charge is dropped, but we still broke jail.'

'That is where you did wrong,' Connie said. She had slipped out of her overcoat. She wore a house dress that accentuated her girlishness. 'You should have waited.'

'Easy to give advice now,' Ed said.

She took it wrong. He had said it jokingly. She flared up, and the colour left her face. Then she saw his smile and the true implication of his words came to her. She sank into a chair.

'Yes,' she said. 'I guess you are right, Ed.'

Big Jim laid his newspaper on the centre table, the paper making a crackling sound. He took off his glasses and put them on the paper. Ed found himself wondering where Mrs. Wilford was. Probably in one of the bedrooms along the long hall, he reasoned. The room was warm. The big hard coal heater, sparkling and shiny with isinglass sides, sent out much heat; the fireplace was loaded with two big logs, and they sputtered and crackled.

'Connie convinced me you never killed Martin Jones,' the cowman said.

Ed glanced at Connie. 'Thanks for the faith in me.' He still could not help being cynical. 'But just the same, Booger Sam an' me are wanted men. We busted jail.'

'Sorry,' Big Jim said. 'But you're right there. I tried to get those charges erased when I withdrew the complaint and killed the warrant. But Sheriff Spears was as stubborn as a Hereford bull in blowfly time. Said it made his office look bad, and he would keep that thousand bucks price out for each of you. I could do nothin' with him.'

'Anyway, the most serious charge is disposed of,' Connie said.

Ed Cotton said, 'And I thank you for that.' His gaze went back to Big Jim Wilford, who was studying him over his pipe. 'Big Jim, who the heck killed this Jones gent, and why?'

'I don't know any more about it then you do, Ed.'

Ed said, 'And I know nothing but that he was found murdered after cuttin' my fence. Somebody is trying to frame me.'

'And it is not the Triangle Diamond,' Connie assured him.

'She is right in that respect,' her father agreed.

Ed again felt puzzled, and this showed in his face with its frost-bitten cheeks. His ride to the Triangle Diamond had not been a complete waste of effort and time, he realized. He had learned that the murder charge had been dropped. That was good. A convicted murderer drew the gallows, and the gallows were only thirteen steps from the noose—steps he had no desire to climb. And he had also got to see Connie again, which was worth riding a thousand miles to accomplish. The word *thousand* reminded him of the reward, and he almost visibly winced.

'I got to keep moving,' he said.

Big Jim asked, 'What do you intend to do?'

'I'm not givin' myself up to the law, I can tell you for sure. I aim to find out who murdered Martin Jones, and why he was murdered. I'm not so interested in the *why* of it as the *who*.'

Big Jim picked up his glasses and readjusted them to his nose. 'Cotton, I almost believe you—even if you did have a fist-fight with Jones down in the El Dorado and each of you swore to kill the other.'

'You don't have to believe me unless you want to, Big Jim.'

91

Connie could see trouble in the offing. 'You had better go, Ed. Dad isn't feeling too well, the doctor says.'

'I can take care of myself, young lady!'

Ed grinned, said, 'So long, people,' and went back through the kitchen, Connie walking behind him but Big Jim remaining in the living room. The kitchen smelled of fresh baked goods—evidently biscuits—and some spice, evidently a cake. Yes, and a roast was in the oven of the huge range. Ed grinned and said, 'Wish I could stay for supper.'

'Some other time, Ed.'

He left her standing beside the window looking out at him, for the window had a storm window on it, and therefore the glass was clear. He went to where Booger Sam waited, and the thought came that he never had found out what Cart Nagle had been doing at the Triangle Diamond. They had had such a short space of time in which to talk that the subject of the gambler—and his visit to the big ranch—had not been mentioned.

But evidently the gambler had come out to see why Big Jim Wilford had withdrawn his murder complaint.

Ed mounted, and he and his partner headed for their rimrock camp where they had their grub cached. The short winter day was drawing to a close. From the valley below them came the bawling of cattle. Triangle

Diamond men were feeding Big Jim's cattle in the feed lots where the snow had been packed down hard from their hoofs.

'Sure glad they dropped that murder charge against you, Looie.'

Ed grinned. 'My neck never would fit into no noose.'

'Sure gonna be a col' night, Looie.'

And it was a cold night, bitterly cold. They fed their horses some oats and picketed them out in the boulders where there was a chance of scraping down the snow and getting a little grass. A horse will paw snow to one side to get at grass, but this a cow will not do. They ate cold beans and melted some snow water for themselves and their mounts, keeping their fire small and hidden in the rocks. The snow had stopped falling. There was no wind. The world was thick with whiteness. There was little if any sleep. They dared not keep the fire lit, for it might disclose their hiding place. They dozed and got cold and walked to keep from freezing to death. And there was in Ed Cotton a terrible, terrible hate. He should have been in his warm cabin, sleeping in his warm bed, his dog on the floor beside him. But somebody had made him an outlaw, a human wolf, a killer.

And that somebody would pay, he vowed grimly.

CHAPTER SEVEN

Dawn finally came. It was cold and ugly and grey. They fried a cottontail rabbit for breakfast and made coffee in the skillet. The warm flesh and the hot coffee did much to repel the cold and to stifle their mean and ugly thoughts.

'Wonder what this day will bring?' mused Booger Sam.

'Don't know,' Ed Cotton grunted. 'But we patrol the fence.'

On that day, Cotton saw a man killed. He had few if any compunctions.

For he figured the man deserved killing.

The two men set an ambush for him and the big coloured man called Booger Sam, and only because they rode the ridges did they discover this ambush. Only because they were higher than those who wanted to kill them did they see the two below them.

These two were the gambler, Cartwright Nagle, and the owner of the El Dorado, Walt Downing.

Ed Cotton and big Booger Sam had been heading toward the Cotton farm, there to watch the spread. They had no particular reason for heading for Ed's farm; they had just patrolled the fence and found it uncut. So they had decided to check on the farm to see if anybody was coming over from the Triangle Diamond to do the chores. Actually Ed hoped that Connie Wilford would ride over to do the chores, and he hoped to see her and talk to her. He wondered if he were in love with Big Jim's daughter. Evidently he was; this made him smile. Connie was the daughter of a cattle king, and was wealthy; he was only a dirt farmer, and a mighty poor one at that. He told himself, Stop dreaming, Ed Cotton. She just feels sorry for you.

Booger Sam said, 'They'll have guards stationed at your spread to watch to see if we ride in, Ed.'

'They might not have.'

The Negro sent him a long slanting look. 'Why do you say that, Ed Cotton?'

'The murder charge is dropped.'

'Yep, but the breakin'-out-of-jail charge is still against us. An' you slugged Rome down into the snow. Course he dunno fer sure who done it, but he'll figure you laid the timber to him.'

'He sure fell,' Ed said, and grinned.

The black man rubbed his face with a mitten. 'My skin is peelin' from this cold. I got a hunch, Ed.'

Ed glanced at him. The shod hoofs of their mounts made crunching sounds on the snow. 'What's the trouble, *compadre*?'

'We should split up an' scout thet place afore we get too close to it. Them boys what is trailin' us has got plenty of savvy. They might set a trap a distance from the spread, you know.'

Ed drew rein, and he felt the flanks of his horse move in and out under his saddle. His horse and that of Booger Sam were getting weary. He wondered idly where they could get new fresh mounts. They could steal some off the Triangle Diamond, leading them out of the barn in the dark. But that would add another charge to their records: horse stealing. And in this country they hanged horse thieves, when and where they caught them. He gave his mind to the idea advanced by Booger Sam.

'Good idea, friend.'

'We'll split up, then, and we'll meet by the big boulder which is down the fence about a mile, behind the hill that hides the house?'

'Suits me.'

And so the hunch of Booger Sam—if hunch it could be called—turned out to be a good one, for they did not ride into the ambush set by Cart Nagle and Walt Downing, there in the timber along the slope of the hill where the spring was. Booger Sam swung his leg-stumbling horse to the east, riding the ridge, and Ed Cotton rode the west ridge, and thus they came in on either side of the men who lay below, expecting them to come along the trail. Nagle had been scouting ahead and his glasses had shown them coming towards the farmhouse, but Ed Cotton and Booger Sam had not seen the gambler because of the high brush. Also, the snow was dazzling white, stretching unbroken for miles except for the tip of dark brush, and this would eventually make a man snow blind.

Nagle had watched, his eyes mean behind his field glasses, and he had identified the pair. So he had led his horse out of the brush, and the hill had hidden him from Ed Cotton and Booger Sam. Then Nagle, following the twisting coulee, his horse breasting snowdrifts in some spots, had ridden back to where Walt Downing sat his bronc, there in the leafless trees that grew around the spring which was now covered with snow and frozen solid to the ground with ice.

'They're ridin' this way, Walt.'

'How far away are they?'

'About a mile and a half, maybe two miles.'

'And they are coming down this trail?'

'Yes, they were—when I saw them.'

Downing was big in his long sheepskin coat. He was thoughtful for a long moment, and the gambler watched him and said nothing.

A magpie chirped, the sound loud in the frozen stillness. He was perched on a scraggly limb, and he watched these two strange things that had invaded his wilderness bailiwick. The scavenger of the range, he was living high now, for cattle were dying in the

97

snow. He cocked his black head with its long glistening beak, and he cawed occasionally to his mate who was in another clump of brush down the coulee.

'That's an awful loud bird,' Cartwright Nagle said angrily. 'Sounds like my first wife, who was always raw hidin' me.'

'Sounds like my third,' Downing said, and grinned. 'Cart, your nerves are shot, man.'

'Ah, go to blazes!'

Downing overlooked the other's anger. He said, 'By rights then they'll ride along the side of yonder hill?'

'They were headed in that direction.'

Downing turned, his overshoes creaking on the snow, and he looked up the opposite slope—the side hill to the west.

'We hide behind them big boulders up there. That means they'll be across the gully from us, and we'll knock them from their saddles with our long-guns.'

'Our broncs? We'll take them with us to them rocks?'

'Yes.'

'We don't want to be too far from our saddle horses,' Cart Nagle said.

'Why so close to them?'

'Ah, don't rib me, Walt. We might have to git out . . . an' git out fast.'

'We won't,' Walt Downing assured him.

They rode their broncs up the slope. They were astraddle grain-fed horses, stout and tough, and the horses took the snow easily, and reached the mess of boulders, scattered there on the hill, some almost covered with snow. The two men rode behind these, and the boulders hid them and their broncs. Downing came down, and he had his Winchester in his hand.

Their horses breathed heavily from their labours. The magpie remained in the leafless trees, and he kept on talking. Walt Downing found himself hating the bird's raucous tongue. He found himself a spot behind a boulder and stamped the snow flat.

'Over there,' he told Nagle.

The gambler moved away and found his spot. The boulder protected him, also; his rifle went over it, and he scraped away snow so the gunsteel would rest on granite. He moved his overshoes. His feet were cold, but they warmed as he spread the snow around, making himself an area where there was sure footing. Then he said, 'They should be comin'.'

'In a little while.'

'We'll wait.'

Downing grinned. 'We have to wait,' he said.

So they settled down and waited, and because of the hunch of a man named Booger Sam their plan was foiled. For behind them came Ed Cotton, and Booger Sam rode the far ridge. They saw Booger Sam first, threading his horse along the tip of the hill where the wind had moved the snow and had laid the ground bare in some spots. Booger Sam was about a quarter of a mile away; the snow was dazzling white, and it made him a hard target. He came over the ridge, and his horse was walking, and the black man had his rifle across the front of his old saddle.

Downing saw him, and surprise flared against his wide face, and the saloon man had a hoarse voice as he said, 'I don't savvy this.'

'He should be riding the draw.'

'And he should have Cotton with him,' Downing said. He turned then and looked up the slope, and as he turned the bullet hit the boulder beside him. It slammed in with evil intent and ricocheted, whining in wild glee across the cold wilderness.

Ed Cotton had fired that bullet.

For a moment, then, there was silence. Walt Downing was aware that the magpie had taken wing and was zooming down the valley in his haste to get beyond rifle range. This was an odd thing. Then the hoarse cry of Cartwright Nagle broke the stillness.

'Man behind us . . . on the slope.'

'Hidden in them boulders,' hollered Walt Downing.

'Git out!'

There was nothing to do but run for their horses and climb into saddles and hope no bullets would cut them or their mounts down.

They had been outmanoeuvred and outguessed; retreat was the only thing left. So they ran for their mounts. Downing was the smarter. He did not climb into his saddle. He hung over his horse, one overshoe in stirrup, and he rode the way a Cheyenne Indian rides—draped over the shoulder of his horse, hanging on to the horn with the body of the horse between him and his enemy. He had to drop his rifle, and this he did without thinking: Then he was riding out and his bronc was running in wild abandon, scared by the bullets. The horse ran down the coulee, and Ed Cotton, who now stood upright, could see only the right hand of Walt Downing as it grabbed the saddle-horn. Ed Cotton had a face as white as the snow. This was an ambush and only by the grace of Sam's hunch had he escaped death. He wanted to kill Downing and he wanted to kill Nagle. But he could not shoot Downing unless he first killed a noble and innocent horse; this he would not do. So he directed his lead toward Nagle, who was not as smart as his boss, for Nagle had climbed astraddle his mount and rode in the saddle. He was bent over, and he brandished his rifle. He was a moving target.

But Nagle was behind Downing.

Ed swung his rifle, and he shot—he missed Cartwright Nagle. Already Downing was beyond the toe of the hill, lost against the boulders. At this moment another rifle came into the battle—the rifle of Booger Sam. And his first bullet dropped Nagle from leather. Nagle had his reins tied, and his horse ran on, leaving his rider in the snow. Then that horse was gone too as the hill hid him from view. And only Nagle was behind, dark and small in the whiteness of the snow.

Ed Cotton ran his bronc along the ridge, and he came to the cut-coulee. Below him were the two horses running toward Greener town. The horse of Nagle, his fright leaving him, stopped and stood against some dead cottonwoods, his run gone—but Downing continued on. Ed shot twice, but the distance was too great, and although he never saw where his bullets landed he knew he had not hit Walt Downing, for he saw Downing swing up and gain his saddle seat. And then the man was pulling out of sight.

He'll report to the sheriff, Ed thought. And he'll tell a big lie. He'll make it look like we ambushed them instead of them ambushing us.

Ed turned his panting horse and rode back to where Nagle lay in the snow. Booger Sam had already reached the man.

'Jes' by luck I hit him, Looie.'

'Is he dead?'

'I dunno. I jes' got here. I ain't had no time to look him over. Downin' got away, huh?'

Ed nodded grimly. 'Prob'ly headin' for the

102

sheriff with a wild cock and bull story.'

'We is further than ever in trouble now, huh?'

Ed could merely nod.

Nagle laid on his belly and the black man rolled him over. He was either dead or unconscious. Ed could not see where the bullet had hit him at first; then he found a hole in the man's sheepskin coat. He opened the coat, and then he saw the blood. The gambler had been shot from behind, and the steel-jacketed bullet had come out through his high ribs over his heart.

'I'll rub his face with snow, Looie.'

Ed said nothing; there was nothing to say. The magpie started chattering again, this time perched in some bullberry bushes. He made a disturbing sound. His mate flew over, gaudy in her black and white coat, and she also started talking. This made it twice as bad. The raucous crowing rubbed like harsh sandpaper on Ed Cotton's nerves. He realized then how close he was to breaking, to letting his nerves take over. With an effort he fought off this feeling. He watched Booger Sam rub snow against Nagle's thin cheekbones. He was surprised when Nagle opened his eyes.

They were dull at first, pasty and sick against the drawn face with its blue whisker roots. Then sanity came to them, and Nagle said, 'I got shot.' And having seemingly verified this fact in his mind, he tried to sit up. This he could not do, and he sank back against the softness of the snow, and his lips were bloodless and cold. His eyes remained open though, moving from man to man and clouded with pain.

'Which one of you shot me?'

'I did,' Booger Sam replied. His thick lips formed words with difficulty. 'You were riding fast. It was a lucky shot.'

'My luck—been muddy lately—'

'Downing pulled out on you,' Ed reminded. 'A fine partner you got, Nagle. How do you feel?'

'Blood on my shirt.'

Ed said, 'Downing dropped his rifle back yonderly.'

'I'll go get it,' Booger Sam said.

The Negro waded through the snow toward the boulders. Ed opened the front of Nagle's shirt. It was a silk shirt, and the man wore long underwear; Ed split these too. The wound was ugly and bloody. Nagle closed his eyes, and his breathing was rapid and hoarse.

Nagle spoke, eyes still closed. 'I got to get to Greener . . . to the doc. You'll help me, Cotton?'

'And get my head in the noose?'

'You got to help me!' Nagle opened his eyes. Suddenly blood moved into his throat and choked him. He sat up and coughed and then went back again, and this time his eyes remained open—but there was nothing in

104

them. They were without thought, without pain. His mouth was open, showing his shiny teeth.

When Booger Sam came wading back, with Downing's rifle in his hand, Ed was pulling down the dead man's eyelids. He had dug in the snow and found a small rock, and he had put this under the dead man's mouth to close it.

'He died, Looie?'

'He's 'dead.'

The Negro crossed himself hurriedly. 'Here is the rifle.'

'Lay it across him.'

'Nice rifle.'

'We don't need it.'

Booger Sam laid the rifle across the dead man, the stock in the snow. Ed felt Nagle's pulse, his fingers on the man's wrist, and he made sure the gambler was dead. Booger Sam watched him, and a question was in his eyes. Ed got to his feet.

'Dead as he'll ever be, Booger.'

'Another black mark on us, Looie. You just got past one murder charge. Now there'll be another out for both of us. Mebbe we should all quit this range.'

'No use trying to get out.'

The Negro rubbed his jaw, and his whiskers made a scratching noise. 'Reckon that's right,' he said. 'Them telegraph wires—they're bad things for a man on the

105

dodge—what does we do with the corpse?'

'Leave him right where he is.'

'Reckon coyotes won't touch him. They're fat an' slick from eatin' so many winter-killed cows. An' they'll come out from town for him. We sure had tough luck.'

'Been tougher if we hadn't followed your hunch.'

'Mah luck runs bad some of the time,' Sam joked, 'but at other times it just runs terrible.'

Ed said, 'We'd best get out of here.'

So they mounted and rode away, leaving the dead gambler in the snow with the Winchester across him, with a rock holding his mouth closed until rigor mortis chilled his blood for the last time.

He glanced at Booger Sam. His eyes met those of the negro.

Booger Sam said, 'Somethin' here I shore don't understand, Looie.'

'An' that?'

'This Downin' fella—he offers to go your bail, remember?'

'Yes, he did. And now he sets an ambush for me. I don't savvy that myself. Maybe he figured the bail was so high he knew darned well I never figured he would raise it—in other words, he just wanted to make a good gesture.'

'But why?'

'I don't know.'

'Maybe he wanted to get you out in the open so he could kill you.'

'I don't see the logic in that.'

'Neither do I. But Nagle an' Rome—they tried to kill you, when they put you under arrest.'

'Sure got a lot of corners I can't see around.'

'What do we do next?'

'I got an idea. It might sound loco as a bull in fly time. But just the same, I got it and I can't get rid of it.'

'Like a balky female, huh?'

'Yep.'

'What is this idea?'

Ed Cotton talked slowly. The wind had arisen again, and he had to ride close to his partner to make himself heard.

'I figure on ridin' into Greener tonight an' havin' a long talk with Sheriff Spears.'

The Negro studied him as though he had made the most foolish statement of his life.

'You mean that, Looie?'

'I sure do.'

'What good with thet do us?'

'I got to talk to somebody. Spears seems to be a fair man. I got to tell him that we had to kill Nagle in defence of our lives; tell him about the ambush set by Downing and Nagle.'

'That won't do no good, way I look at it.'

'Somethin' is haywire here. Ever since I

107

fenced the Canyon, I've had trouble. It relates in some manner to Black Canyon. My fences have been cut in the Canyon, and why I don't know.'

'But what if we get caught down in Greener? It will mean the gallows, what with this gambler bein' kilt.'

'We got to chance it.'

'Well, wait until night comes.'

From a high ridge they watched a bobsled come out from Greener and make a wide circle at the point where Nagle lay; they watched four men load the dead man into the rig. The snow was falling now and the wind had covered their tracks. They were about a mile away from the bobsled, which was pulled by two black horses. Ed could not clearly recognize the men. But one of them, he felt sure, was Sheriff Spears.

'Those men had a hard time findin' the carcass,' Booger Sam said. 'Reckon thet rifle barrel stickin' up thataway showed them where it was, 'cause by now the snow has covered him.'

'And covered our tracks, too.'

The body loaded into the box, the bobsled started back toward Greener, horses trotting. Evidently the men considered it time wasted to look for tracks. There were four saddled horses tied to the bobsled, a pair on each side. Evidently had they been able to find tracks they would have done some riding. Ed knew that the snow was rough on him and Booger, but yet the snow was an asset, a friend. He thought wryly it was the only friend they had. Then he thought of Connie Wilford.

They hunkered in the boulders, walking occasionally to restore circulation. The day was short, as are all winter days on a northern range. They headed for Greener at about six that evening. They met one man on the ride to the cow town. This man did not see them, for they were hidden in some timber when he passed; the man plodded along carrying a rifle, and he had a pack on his back. Across one shoulder were some blankets, strapped over the buckskin pack. He went steadily across the snow, and he wore snowshoes. He was headed north along the rim of Black Canyon.

'Do my eyes see rightly, Looie?'

'Who do you think he is?'

'Cain't be nobody but thet game warden, thet Faver fellow. Light is bad—almost dark—but it sure looks like him.'

Ed Cotton lowered the glasses. He was frowning. Faver seemed to fit in somewhere—but at what point? The man was a riddle. Here he was scouting Black Canyon, bent against the snow and the wind, when he could have been down in his home in Greener enjoying the fireplace and his family. Something big was in the air . . . something he could not see. Then Game Warden Curt

Faver was out of sight, a part of the night and its silken mystery.

And Ed Cotton said, 'Us for Greener and a talk with Spears.'

CHAPTER EIGHT

Spears had been sheriff for more years than he cared to remember. Sometimes when he looked back on life it seemed to him he had been sheriff all his days, he had held the office so long. He had reared a family of three boys and two girls, and now they had left and he and his wife were alone. He had never gotten along too well with his missus, who was a finicky person who had, at one time early in their marriage, tried to get him to remove his boots before coming into the house—she wanted no dirt or dust in her home! But this had been a step too far, and many times the sheriff had deliberately dirtied his boots before entering, just to show her he was the boss.

When the trouble had broken loose, his wife had sent a man to the railroad and this man had in turn sent a wire to the sheriff, and this had brought him home. He had questioned Deputy Sheriff Fred Rome at great length, thereby angering the deputy. He did not like Rome too well, but his wife had almost made him hire the man as a deputy, for at that time he had had a wife and a child. But the wife had soon left him—taking the child with her. And Mrs. Spears had lost one of her best friends, and her husband had got stuck with Rome as a deputy. Sometimes he figured he should discharge the arrogant deputy.

He did not like to have Rome hang around the El Dorado Saloon. It didn't look good for a member of the law to stick around the saloon. He realized he knew little about Fred Rome. He had been one of the four men who had gone out after Nagle's body. Rome had grumbled, 'We might find their tracks, if we headed out along the ridges,' but he had vetoed that as being foolish. Rome seemed to want to get a rifle against Ed Cotton; he seemed to want to kill Cotton.

He had questioned Walt Downing about the shooting. According to Downing, he and Nagle had been riding along, and Ed Cotton and the crazy Negro had jumped them and had shot down Nagle. Sheriff Spears had asked if Downing wanted to file a murder charge against either Cotton or the Negro, but Downing had made no reply to this. The whole thing was a puzzle to the lawman. He was musing about it now as he sat in his office playing whist with the jailer, who was still grumbling about the jail delivery engineered by Booger Sam.

111

'I'd sure like to lay my shotgun acrost thet black man's skull,' the jailer grumbled. 'Your play, Spears.'

'That black man would break your back with one hand,' the sheriff joked. 'He'd snap you in two like a lead pencil.'

'Not me he wouldn't.'

'You're so mad you made a bad play.'

'I'm not mad.'

So the talk had gone back and forth. Sheriff Spears intended to spend the night in his office. He didn't want to go home. Since the children had grown and had left home, his wife was even harder to live with. When the children had been around, she nagged them; now they were gone and all her efforts were concentrated on him. His office was warm and the bunk looked good. He thought of Ed Cotton and the Negro. They would love to have a warm bunk. He had to get them, he realized. He liked Ed Cotton. Hard worker, that young man—a brave man, too, settling on Big Jim Wilford's range like that.

Cotton did not seem to be the type who would shoot a man from ambush, as they claimed he had shot down Martin Jones. Nor did he seem to be the type to pack a grudge. He and Jones had fought fair and square that night in the El Dorado. Some claimed Martin Jones had even forced the fight—had gone out of his way to pick trouble with the farmer. Jones was not much of a hand, Spears

112

figured. He had stuck around the saloon when he should have been out riding range for his boss. But Jones was out of this now . . . for good.

He wished he could have a talk with Ed Cotton. This thought playing idly in his mind, he returned his attention to the whist game. He hated cards of all sorts. But there was nothing to do but play whist this cold blustery winter night. So he had agreed to play with the jailer. The jailer had had a rough time the last few days. Some of the citizens had joshed him about losing his prisoners. Some had even gone so far as to say jokingly he had deliberately turned them loose. Some had claimed a man his age should be retired to the rocking-chair. And the jailer had spent some tough moments arguing with his tormentors.

Sheriff Spears soon had his wish. He soon was talking with Ed Cotton. At this moment, Ed and his Negro pal were riding into Greener. The town was a blur of lights in the falling snow, but back of each light was warmth—a hot stove filled with good lignite coal. The sight of the lights in homes did Ed not a bit of good, nor did it bring cheer to Booger Sam.

'We're jes' on the wrong side of them lights, Looie.'

'You're a cheerful cuss.'

'I'm a cold cuss, Ed.'

113

They rode down the alley behind the El Dorado. Evidently there was a card game in progress in the El Dorado's back room, for there was a lamp lit there—the dim rays tried to penetrate the frosted-over windows, and almost failed.

Across town, a dog barked. He sounded mournful and lonely. No dogs answered him; not even a coyote yelped. Ed did not know what feelings were running through his big and bony partner, but he knew he was filled with tension and apprehension. Maybe this ride was no good. Maybe they were doing wrong. They were riding into the enemy's stronghold. Maybe the night would be shattered by sullen red gunfire.

They came to the back of the jail. Ed dismounted and looked up at Booger Sam, who sat his saddle and had made no move to leave his horse.

'I'll hide our horses in thet barn over yonder, Looie.' The Negro's mittened hand designated the open door of an old building directly behind the jail. 'I'll watch our backs.'

'Good idea.'

The Negro led the horses into the barn, dismounting in front of the door. Ed went between two buildings and reached Greener's main drag. For a long moment he stood hidden and watched the silent town. But he saw no enemy—nobody moved on the strip—so he walked boldly around the corner

114

and went to the door of the sheriff's office, where he knocked and waited. His heart was a triphammer tring to smash his ribs.

'Who's there?'

The voice, he decided, belonged to Sheriff Spears. He wished the windows had not been frosted over, for then he could have glanced into the office.

'Big Jim Wilford,' he replied, trying to imitate the cowman's deep voice.

There was a moment of silence. He heard a man move, heard a chair being pushed back. The silence seemed very long. He glanced up and down the street, and his glance was hurried. He saw nothing that prophesied danger. He put one mitten in his sheepskin pocket and held his .45 rigid.

'Jes' a minute, Big Jim.'

His ruse had worked; elation ran through him. He heard the bolt slide, and the door opened.

Two strides, and he was inside. One hand went behind him, shutting the door. His gun was solid and it covered the two men. The jailer had opened the door. He stepped back, and his face was the colour of a buckskin horse. His mouth jerked, quivered; words spilled from him.

'Cotton! Comin' to give yourself up, eh?'

Ed grinned bleakly. 'With a gun in my hand?' He looked at Sheriff Spears. The sheriff still held on to his composure. He had

115

turned in his swivel chair slightly. He was looking at his six-shooter which hung from the coat rack. It was too far away, so he glanced hurriedly at his rifle which leaned in the corner. Then he gave up these thoughts and looked at Ed.

'What's on your mind, Cotton?'

Ed didn't answer. His .45 made a solid quick gesture. 'Sit down, jailer,' he ordered. 'And make it soon, for I have no time to lose.'

On wooden legs, the jailer moved to his chair. He settled in it very slowly. He seemed to be afraid to lower his weight into the chair suddenly. Finally he managed to settle down.

'You'll pay for this, Cotton,' he croaked.

Ed disregarded this. He leaned against the wall; from this point he could watch both men, and if somebody barged through the door he would be behind the man who entered.

'You're holding a gun on the law,' Spears said slowly.

Ed nodded. 'I know that, and I'm sorry, Spears. I like you. But I have to play my cards close. I came to tell you that Downing and Nagle set an ambush trap for me and my partner. By luck we rode around it instead of into it. We killed Nagle, but we did it in defence of our lives.'

'Downing gives a different version,' the sheriff said, reaching for his pipe. He got it between his teeth and tried to light it, but it had no tobacco. His eyes were sharp and speculative. He laid the pipe down. 'Downing claims you two jumped him an' Nagle and they had to fight for their lives.'

'Downing lies.'

The sheriff pushed tobacco into his pipe. 'Your word against his.'

'I have a witness. He hasn't.'

'But the word of your witness would be no good in a court of law. Your witness is a wanted man, and the charge is engineering a jail break.'

'Did Downing swear out a murder charge against us?'

'No . . .'

The jailer moved in his chair. He was as squirming as a schoolboy in the principal's office. He wet his lips, and Ed swung his .45 back to cover the sheriff, who now had his pipe going.

'Why don't you give yourself up, Cotton?' Spears asked quietly.

Ed smiled at that. 'Somebody wants me off this range. Somebody has cut my fence and somebody murdered Martin Jones. I think they wanted Jones out of the way, too, just like they wanted me. So they decided to kill two birds with one stone.'

'I think your imagination is running away with you,' the lawman said, pulling on his pipe.

'My fence has been cut a number of times.'

'Big Jim Wilford isn't responsible for what his cowpunchers do. They hate barbed wire, just like every range hand hates it.'

'There's more than that.'

Again the lawman asked, 'Give yourself up. I'll see you get a fair deal, Cotton.'

'A cell?'

'Yes, I'd have to jail you.'

'And you know what would happen?' Ed Cotton answered his own question. 'Somebody would sneak in and murder me. Shoot me down like a canary in his cage.'

'I'd post a guard. Twenty-four hours a day.'

Ed smiled. 'I'm not takin' that chance. I was in jail once. When a man is in jail, he's terribly helpless. This deputy of yours—this Fred Rome fellow—he tried to drive me into a gunfight.'

'Rome tells differently. He claims you got belligerent and wouldn't submit to arrest.'

'He lies.'

The sheriff made sucking sounds. 'Why would Rome be against you, Cotton?'

'I don't know. But I do know one thing—he is against me.'

'Your imagination again.'

Ed said, 'We're gettin' nowhere in a hurry. But I want you to patrol my fence and find out who is cutting it in Black Canyon, and why it is being cut. All I ask is a fair shake.'

'You're getting a fair deal, and you'll

continue to get a fair deal. Just lay down that gun and give yourself up, huh?'

Ed shook his head.

'I'm after you—the minute you leave here.'

Ed said, 'That's your job.' He was really putting Spears on the spot. Word would get around that a hunted man had deliberately ridden into Greener and had thrown down on the sheriff, and that would not look good for Sheriff Spears. Lamplight shone from the brass fittings on the jailer's red braces. The lamplight showed the high cheekboned face of the sheriff. Ed realized his visit had done no good. He had to get out of Greener. The stove was warm and the room and walls turned the snow. For a moment he almost wavered, remembering the coldness of the rimrock. But then he thought of the bars and the little slot where the food was shoved in on a tray, and he knew he would rather die a free wolf than to have a chain and collar.

He reached back and got the door knob. 'So long,' he said, and he darted out into the storm. He did not wait to hear if there was any commotion in the little office. He knew that the jailer and the sheriff would run for their weapons. So he wasted no time.

He ran around the corner and came out on the alley. Booger Sam had heard the door slam and had their broncs ready, and Ed vaulted into his saddle despite the weight of his overcoat and the hindrance of his cumbersome overshoes. He turned his horse and rode into the snow-filled night. Behind him he heard the jail door open, but he knew the sheriff would not follow him. The snow was a protective blanket. Spears could ride past them a dozen feet away, and still not see them because of the snow. Ed therefore did not ride fast; there was no need for speed. He kept his horse at a trot. Behind him rode Booger Sam. Suddenly Ed's bronc shied. Something ahead had scared him. Ed pulled in and leaned forward and looked into the night. The back door of the El Dorado was open, and he could barely see the dog team and sled there. Their horses had smelled the dogs, and that had kept them from riding down on the team. Ed pulled his bronc into a vacant lot and rode across it, coming out on Montana Street. There was no hollering or noise behind them. Evidently the sheriff and jailer had come out, had seen the thick snowfall, and had decided against trying to follow them. Ed pulled in his horse.

'Did you see what I saw?'

'Dog team, looked like.'

'They were unloading the sled, weren't they?'

They had to keep their heads close together to make themselves heard. The wind sang in the leafless cottonwood trees and in the eaves of the buildings.

'I dunno whether they were loading it or

unloading it, Looie.'

Ed said, 'In the night, they have a dog team come in. This I don't savvy, Booger.'

'Neither do I. Sure seems odd thet men will drive dogs, an' not hosses.' The Negro stirred in his saddle. 'Sure cold. You got somethin' on your mind asides your muskrat cap, Looie?'

'I'm going back there.'

'Why?'

'Scout aroun'.'

'I'll stay with the horses.'

Ed dismounted and walked back to the alley. He came in along the buildings and was soon in the area back of Downing's saloon. But now there was no dog team. Only the snow, falling across the light of the window. He was mystified. The dog team had left. This he could not understand. He was getting cold again—the coldness was sharp and was penetrating his sheepskin coat. The brief visit to the sheriff's office had warmed him for the first time in days. But this was beside the point. Why were they unloading—or loading—furs at night? Suddenly he remembered a man plodding through the snow, bent over under the weight of his pack. A man who should have been at home with his family around a hot stove was out in the wilderness. Game Warden Curt Faver.

Ed thought, Nothing I can do here, and he was turning to go when the back door of the

121

El Dorado, about forty feet away, suddenly opened. Two men came out in their shirt sleeves. This told him they did not intend to stay long in the cold. The door was left open behind them and the lamplight streamed out to show them clearly. They crossed the alley and came to the storehouse there. Ed saw one of them tug at the lock, as though to make sure it was fast.

'I told you I snapped that lock,' Walt Downing said angrily.

Fred Rome had been the man who had tested the lock. 'Jes' wanted to make sure, Walt.'

'You sure now?'

'The door is locked.'

'Then let's get back inside and continue our game. Man alive, you got more troubles than an ol' maid.'

They returned to the El Dorado. The door went shut and the stream of light stopped.

Ed Cotton added up what he had seen. There was apparently only one conclusion to be reached. Evidently the warehouse held something of great value. Ed knew that whisky was stored out there, but was the fear that whisky would be stolen so strong that it took two men out into the cold night to make sure the lock was snapped securely?

This did not seem logical.

Also, Deputy Sheriff Fred Rome had been with Walt Downing. Rome had been the one who had been afraid the lock had not been secured. This did not make sense. The storehouse did not belong to Rome. It belonged to Downing. Ed shivered as the cold cut into him. He could have gone forward, gun in hand, and made them open the storehouse. But what good would that have done him? He went back to where Booger Sam and the horses waited. The Negro had dismounted, and he was walking in a circle to keep warm, leading their tired mounts. His gun was in his hand as Ed materialized out of the storm.

Ed told him what he had seen and heard.

'An' thet dog team . . . it was gone, huh?'

'Gone like the world had swallowed it. And they came out and looked at the lock on the door.'

'Wonder what thet storehouse holds?'

'You stay here. I'm goin' back.'

'Looie, we should hightail out of this town.'

'I'll only be gone a minute.'

'Well, okay.'

Ed moved again into the night. He sidled close to the storehouse door and felt the lock. It was a heavy lock, and the hasp was heavy and strong, bolted into the thick plank door and the door jamb. He went completely around the building, which was made of logs. It had small windows—so small a man could not crawl through them, even had the bars been ripped from them. It had no back door. He was baffled, and he wished he had a crowbar to break the lock from the hasp.

But he had no bar.

He could do nothing but return to Booger Sam. When he came to the Negro, the black man said, 'We need fresh hosses, Looie.'

'Let's steal some out of the livery barn.'

'We'll do thet. What did you find out?'

Ed told him about the locked door, the small windows, and that the storehouse had no back door. They were going down an alley, leading their hungry, weary animals.

'Looked to me, Ed, like them men was either loadin' or unloadin' bales of somethin', which could be furs.'

'I don't understand this,' Ed said.

The Negro had no answer to this. They came to the back door of the town livery stable. Ed hoped that the door would not be bolted from inside. He pushed it, hoping to slide it on its overhead rollers; the door held. He pushed harder. The door moved and the hinges creaked as the rollers moved along the cold steel channels. But the door was not locked, which was a bit of luck for them. The owner of the barn was an old broken-down cowpuncher, and he slept in a small room close to the front door. He had a bunk and a stove there, and most of the time he was saturated with whisky. There was no light in the room. Overhead hung a kerosene lantern,

124

its chimney black with soot. Because of the dirty chimney, the lantern cast very little light. There were not many horses in the barn—nine to be exact—so they had little choice. Ed did not like to have to steal a fresh horse. After this was over, there would be another charge against him and Booger, and he remembered wryly that they hanged horse thieves in this section of the cow-country. But their lives depended on good horseflesh. So they had no other choice.

'I'll take thet big roan over there,' Booger said hoarsely.

'Not so loud, man.'

'Mah voice . . . I cain't talk low, Looie.'

'Then learn how!'

Ed realized he had spoken sharply to his companion. He felt sorry immediately. He stripped the saddle and bridle off his tired horse and led out a raw-boned sorrel that bore Big Jim Wilford's brand. Evidently one of the Triangle Diamond hands was spending the night in Greener. The dim lantern light showed that Booger Sam's roan also packed the Triangle Diamond iron. That meant that two Triangle Diamond men were in town, and come morning they would ride into the big spread on the horses he and Booger Sam were discarding. The thought came that Big Jim might not file a complaint against them for horse stealing. And then again, he might . . . But maybe Connie would intercede on

125

their behalf. That was a good thought. Oh, well, he thought, we'll see what we'll see.

He laid his saddle blanket across the sorrel's back and slowly lifted his saddle. The sorrel was a bigger horse, so he had to let out the latigo on the off-side; this took some time, for the tongue of the cinch buckle seemed reluctant to leave the thick leather of the latigo strap. Booger Sam had already saddled and was cramming the bit into the mouth of his new mount. He had to lengthen his headstall, and he fumbled with the buckle. Suddenly he stiffened. For from the office had come the sound of a man coughing. The sound was loud in the silence. Ed Cotton whispered, 'The hostler. Too many cigarettes.'

'Let's get out of here.'

They did not tie their mounts in the stalls. They left them free. The horses of their own accord walked into the stalls and started eating the hay out of the mangers. Ed and his partner led their broncs toward the open back door. Although the interior of the barn was cold, it was much colder outside. Ed slid the door shut, and the rollers seemed to howl. Suddenly from the front of the barn came a sleepy voice.

'Somebody out there?'

The old hostler had evidently been completely awakened by the squeal of the rollers in their troughs. But Ed already had the door shut. He went into saddle, and he and his partner loped away into the storm. The thick snow muffled the sounds left by their horses' steel-shod hoofs. Ed's horse was fresh and he wanted to run, so Ed Cotton let him out; beside him rode Booger Sam on his fresh mount. They rode into the swift-falling snow and were out of Greener in hardly any time at all. About a mile out of town they pulled down their mounts to a trot. They had to conserve horseflesh.

'Wonder if thet ol' buzzard checked on the hosses in the barn?' Booger Sam hollered.

'Makes no never-mind,' Ed replied.

'No, reckon it don't. Feels good to have a hard hoss atween my laigs again, Looie.'

'Cold night.'

'They're all cold.'

They headed for the rimrock camp, which would be hard to find in the dark. Ed's memory went back to their visit in Greener. His talk with Sheriff Spears had netted him nothing. Or had he made some impression on the lawman? He did not know. Downing and Rome had either been loading furs on the sled, there in the alley, or they had been unloading them. He was not sure. Then he realized they must have just finished unloading the dog sled, for they later checked on the lock on the storehouse.

There was something big here.

He aimed to find out what it was, even if it

cost him his life.

CHAPTER NINE

Ed Cotton slept little that night. A man cannot sleep soundly when he is out in a blizzard, even though when he awakened he was covered by protective snow. A thousand things bothered him. He was dog-tired, and when he did sleep he slept in snatches. His feet were ice cold, despite his heavy socks and liners and overshoes. The little sleep he got was filled with bad dreams. He was worried about his stock. He was running out of hay. This cold spell had lasted a long time, and he had not cut much hay—the summer had been dry and hay had not grown very tall. Booger Sam lay close to him. He did not sleep well either. He rolled and tossed, mumbling to himself. For some time Ed lay awake, covered by snow. He had dragged the coloured man into this, and for that he was sorry. Then the full realization of Booger's steadfastness came to him and filled him with pride. Booger Sam was indeed a true friend.

His mind returned to his cattle. With snow so deep and with blizzard after blizzard sweeping this high range, his cattle could not forage. They would have to be fed twice a day. Had not Connie Wilford taken this chore upon her pretty shoulders, his cattle would have died. He owed an awful lot to Big Jim Wilford's daughter, and to Booger Sam.

Finally he struggled up out of the snow. He spent the remainder of the night with his back against a rough boulder. Occasionally he walked and stamped his feet to restore circulation. His mind went to Connie Wilford. She would be sleeping in a warm bedroom. In his mind's eye he could envision her lovely hair draped over the snow white pillowcase. Why did he stay on this snow-bound range?

Was it because of his property—his cattle and his farm? Yes, in part—in large part. Was it because of Connie? Yes, to a degree—maybe a larger degree than he cared to admit, even to himself.

But there was another reason, too—the big reason. He was not going to be chased off any range. A man had to have his pride, or he had nothing.

He found himself dozing. Without knowing it, he slipped into a deep sleep. This time the sleep was disturbed only by the cold. When he awakened he was deadly cold. Booger Sam slept in the snow, and Ed could hear his snores. He did not awaken the Negro. Booger Sam could sleep any place and at any time. The sun finally came through the heavy clouds, for it had stopped snowing. It was not much of a sun; it held no warmth. It was cold and brassy and distant in the thick sky. Ed jabbed Booger Sam with his elbow, and the Negro struggled up out of the snow.

'I was dreamin' of pickin' cotton along the Gulf. By golly, I was warm, too, but I ain't no longer.'

'No longer what?' Ed joked.

'No longer warm, Looie.'

Ed said, 'Let's have breakfast, huh?'

'Serve it to this boy in bed?'

'Sure,' Ed said, 'sure.'

Ed opened a can of beans with his pocket-knife. He had held the can close to his body inside his overcoat for an hour or so to put some heat into it. Even at that he had to cut the beans out of the can. They dared not light a fire because the snow had ceased falling and the smoke could have been seen for miles, and the smoke would have betrayed their hiding place. They got outside of the beans, and Booger Sam said, 'Sure wish I had that ceegar.'

'Wish for the moon,' Ed replied.

'You ain't very congenial this fine warm mawnin', Looie.'

'Beat me,' Ed said, and grinned.

They finished their 'breakfast' and mounted and rode toward Ed's farm, and there in the high pines they watched the law change guards. Two men rode out from Greener, and a man came out of the barn and another out of the house, and they talked to

130

the new guard for a while before riding back to town. They would get warm breakfasts. Bacon fried just right—crisp bacon—and gallons of scalding hot coffee and a stack of golden brown hotcakes, melting the butter and covered with syrup.

'I been thinkin' about thet game warden, Edward.'

'He ain't thinkin' about you.'

'He's wrapped up in this somewhere. I remember that dog sled and them men unloadin' bales of somethin', which I think was furs.'

'Faver is on the trail of something,' Ed had to admit. 'Furs might be tied up in this. Beaver are worth a fortune now.'

They watched the two guards disappear in the distance. The two new fresh guards both went into the house. Ed Cotton figured the guard had stayed in the barn overnight to make sure he and Booger Sam didn't sneak down and steal fresh saddle horses—the guards' own horses. This made Ed smile a little, and the thought came that he could not remember far enough back to recall the last time he had smiled. And this thought was not good.

An hour later, two riders came from the direction of Big Jim Wilford's Triangle Diamond outfit. Glasses showed them to be Connie and a man, evidently one of the Triangle Diamond riders.

'They're talkin' to them guards,' Booger Sam said.

Ed said, 'Betcha they got a handful of news to spill to her, seein' we left our broncs in the livery and borrowed two of her ol' man's horses.'

'Big Jim might not care too much.'

'Let's hope so.'

Connie and the cowpuncher went to the hay corral and started doling hay over the five-wire fence to Ed's cattle and horses. Ed watched and saw they did not overfeed; Connie knew just the right amount of hay to feed to keep a cow or horse on his feet. She knew cattle and horses, Ed realized.

'No use us stayin' here, Looie. Ah'm cold.'

'I've been cold all my life,' Ed grunted.'

They decided to ride the high ridges, keeping hidden by the pine and spruce, and to look at the fences. They did not dare ride openly along the fences; they were patrolled by riders. Therefore they had to scrutinize the fence through the field glasses, and this was difficult indeed. The sun made the snow dazzling white, and it is almost impossible to see shiny barbed wire from a distance of a quarter mile or so. They finally gave the task up as impossible. About an hour later, they saw two riders; they were pushing toward the Wilford ranch. The glasses showed one of them to be Sheriff Spears. But at first Ed could not recognize the other rider, and he handed the glasses to Booger Sam, who took off his right mitten and slowly turned the focusing screw down to make the lenses fit his eyes.

Ed watched the black face, stern and unrelenting. Then the Negro handed the glasses back and put on his mitten again.

'Thet other gent looks like the jailer.'

'Either that, or the old hostler in the livery barn.'

'Prob'ly the livery barn man, an' they is ridin' out to tell Big Jim we borrowed two of his hosses.'

They watched the pair ride out of sight over a hill, and then they continued their patrolling. Riders came from the west, and they hid out; the riders went past them, not seeing them. This range was spiked with short-guns and rifles.

Ed found himself thinking of Curt Faver.

'Let's try to find Faver,' he said.

'What good will that do us?'

'He isn't patrollin' hills for his health, not in this cold weather. He's on to somethin'—somethin' big.'

The big dark eyes studied him. The thick lips moved slowly. 'Might be a good idea, Looie.'

Ed smiled. 'Maybe the best I've had all day, huh?'

'All week, you mean.'

Curt Faver had spent his life in the wilderness. He had long been with the U.S. government in game protection jobs. Now he held two jobs. He was a state game warden, in addition to drawing a salary from Uncle Sam. He had worked in game protection from the Mexican Border to the Canadian Line. He liked the southern part of the United States best because of the warm climate, but Uncle Sam had years before moved him north, and he had undertaken the chore without grumbling. He had often asked for transfers out of this cold section, but the bosses in Washington had never favoured his pleas. So he had decided long ago to make the best of it.

He had watched the trouble between Ed Cotton and the law with impartial eyes. He was not a lawman except where illegal trapping was concerned. His business was to ride herd over wild game: elk and deer and moose and mink and beaver and other fur-bearing animals. He issued hunting permits, and when a man could prove beaver were causing damage to his property by cutting down timber or building dams that held back water which flooded hay meadows and grain fields, then he issued a permit to catch a certain number of the beaver. But he seldom issued such permits, because beaver were still scarce and breeding stock had to be preserved, or the beaver would become extinct.

The last few months had been busy months for Curt Faver, for reports had come out from Washington, D.C., that illegally trapped beaver pelts were coming on to the eastern markets. These reports had been handed in by legitimate fur companies in the central and southern and northern states—companies who had been approached to buy illegally trapped beaver. Each legally trapped pelt had to have a government and state stamp on it, telling the name of the trapper and where the pelt had been caught. These dealers had in return reported to the bigwigs in Washington, and the reports had gone west to various game wardens.

Government men had laboriously traced the fur shipments to this section of Montana, and the home office had even sent out a young game warden to help him. This young man was named Aloysius Smith, Jr. He had just graduated from cow college. He was green as spring grass. He couldn't take the wilderness trails, even though he had played tackle on the college eleven. So Faver had left him in Greener to do the book work. Aloysius Smith, Jr., now sat in a warm office. Faver wanted him there—this was a one man game. Faver knew this range. He knew what creeks held the beaver and he knew just about what the beaver population of any particular stream was. Greener was close to the Canadian Line, and he feared beaver pelts were being smuggled into the area from Canada.

These particular beaver pelts had come from an area that was very cold. This was determined by the thickness of the under-pelt and the length of the hairs. Suspicion pointed toward Greener.

Ten years before, beaver had been on the verge of becoming extinct. Trappers had moved into the West and had trapped beaver to the point where it was feared that the broad-tailed water animal would be no more. Therefore strict state and government laws had been passed to protect this animal that was so easy to trap. And Curt Faver had been singled out as one of the men to see that these laws were closely observed. But this area was miles in width and length, and patrolling all streams was indeed a difficult chore. A man couldn't be every place at the same time.

The last few years had really seen the beaver colonies grow in size. Dams had been built by the busy animals, and they had bred and their numbers had rapidly increased. But now somebody was trapping them, and somebody was becoming rich. Faver's job was to find out who that somebody was.

He had issued a few permits to trappers, but these permits did not cover the entire amount of hides being shipped out to illegitimate fur buyers.

Curt Faver was a quiet man. He was close-mouthed. He did not even let his wife know about this trouble he was facing. She had thought it odd that the government had sent in Aloysius Smith, Jr., but at her inquiry, Faver had told her that Junior was just checking his books—a usual government procedure. And she had believed this, and had asked no more questions.

Letter after letter had demanded more speed in apprehending the poachers. These letters had come from both governmental and state offices. Faver had not read some of them. He had merely thrown them in the pot-bellied heater and had watched them burn and curl and become ashes. He had played cards in the El Dorado, and he had kept his mouth shut and his eyes and ears open. He had scouted creeks, and he had found no traps. He knew he was being scouted in return—he knew that eyes always watched him from the high hills.

He knew this because once or twice he had caught sight of his trailers. But he knew the wilderness and its trails, and he had lost them by manoeuvring through the hills. He also knew who and what was behind Ed Cotton's troubles. He was sure also that soon fur would be moved out of Greener. Two shipments had already gone out, spaced about two weeks apart. He had tried to waylay each of them, and he had failed.

The first time, he had watched Black Canyon, and the fur shipment had gone out through Rocky Gorge, to the east. The second time he had watched Rocky Gorge, and the fur had gone out of the country via Black Canyon. He had entertained this thought: He would station Mr. Aloysius Smith, Jr., at one point, watching one canyon, and he would watch the other. But then he decided against this because Smith did not know this wilderness, nor did he know the ways and methods of beaver poachers. Besides, he might get killed.

So he had decided to work alone.

He did not know that he had been seen by Booger Sam and Ed Cotton the evening before, when they had been riding toward Greener. He had built a lean-to shelter on the ridge overlooking Rocky Gorge and he had hiked to this in the storm, picking his way the way a wolf finds his goal in a storm—more by instinct than by landmarks. He had built the lean-to out of pine trees and had covered the sloping roof with boughs of spruce and pine. The area had been almost snowed in. But he made camp here—not a warm camp, but a reliable camp. When morning came, he was cold to the marrow of his tough bones. Before Ed Cotton had got into trouble, Game Warden Curt Faver had had the mountains and rangelands all to himself. But such was the case no longer.

For with a bounty on the head of Ed Cotton, with bounty money resting on the curly thatch of one Booger Sam, the hills had become filled with riders. Riders who were half-drunk, cold, and trigger-happy. Riders who would shoot at any man on foot in the hope he was either Cotton or Booger Sam. Or, for that matter, shoot at a man on horseback.

The first day of the manhunt, one of the drunks had shot a deer. A doe. Faver had caught him riding away from the warm carcass. He had taken the man to Greener and had thrown him into jail. He also had had a run-in with Fred Rome. Rome had protected the man saying that the rider had thought he had shot at a man in the brush. And Faver had really poured it on. He had also reported the case to Sheriff Spears after the sheriff had arrived on the scene. Spears had pulled back some of the riders. The county supervisors were picking on Spears, too. He had hired too many men to look for Cotton and Booger Sam. The chase was costing too much money. Rome had really hired the additional deputies, but Spears got the blame. So Spears in turn had jumped on Rome.

Faver built a small fire, using twigs he gathered under a pine tree. He had a frying pan and some bacon. He made coffee in the pot he had cached at the shelter. He scouted once, and saw two riders in the distance. They would see the smoke of his fire. His glasses, trained on the two, made them clear enough for identificaton, and he went back to his culinary chores.

Booger Sam had been the first to spot the smoke—the slow tendril hanging against the sky, there on the ridge. And he had pulled in his borrowed horse, his mittened hand rising to point.

'Somebody has got a campfire up there, Looie, boy.'

Ed Cotton had squinted and had finally picked out the light blue ribbon, there against the grey sky.

'Now who would that be?' the Negro questioned.

Ed did some thinking. 'Wouldn't be a member of this two-bit posse. Them boys don't cook out in the badlands; they eat nice warm meals on the county down in the café.'

'I'd say off-hand it was this game warden gent.'

'Hardly could be anybody else,' Ed replied. 'An' he was aheadin' in this direction when we saw him last night.'

'Let's scout the ridge, huh?'

'All right.'

They came in behind Curt Faver's camp. After hiding their horses, they dismounted and went ahead on foot carrying their rifles. Ed was the first to get to the camp. Faver was frying bacon in the pan. Ed could smell the bacon—the smell was sweet and his belly almost revolted. He came out of the buckbrush with his Winchester half-raised and said, 'Curt Faver, stay where you are, and forget you own a gun.'

Faver said nothing. He turned his head, and a grin cut across his thin face. His words were dry and low.

'Been expectin' you, Cotton. Saw you two boys down below, and then you suddenly disappeared, and I knew my fire had attracted your attention.'

Ed was surprised. 'You built the fire to lure us in huh?'

'I did.'

'You got a trap set for us?'

'No, I'm alone.'

'Then why do you want to see us?'

The bacon sizzled. The aroma was even sweeter now, for Ed Cotton was closer to the fire. So far Booger Sam had not made his exit from the brush. Booger Sam would be playing it cautious. Ed figured his partner was within ear shot. He waited for the game warden's next words.

'I think we can work together, Cotton. I need some hands on this job.'

'What job?'

'The job I'll explain if you'll lower that rifle, come in and sit and drink some coffee and get outside of some bacon. Yes, and call

141

your pard out of the brush, huh? I don't like a rifle on my spine.'

'Come on out, Booger.'

The Negro came out of the brush. He was grinning. 'Man alive, is that pork hawg I done smells?'

'That's right,' said Faver.

The Negro moved over, snowshoes crackling on the snow, and he looked into the frying pan, tiny tendrils of smoke moving across his dark face.

'You got enough there for three hungry men, Mistuh Faver.'

Faver smiled. 'I cooked enough for three men,' he informed him. 'I figured you boys would call on me.'

'Let's tie into it,' Booger Sam said.

Curt Faver had to fry another pan of bacon. Ed Cotton and Booger Sam ate like men who were starving. They emptied one coffee pot and they boiled another. They put it in the snow to cool it, for they had no cups and had to drink out of the pot. Finally they had to stop eating. They had talked little during the repast, for talking interfered with their eating. And they had to watch the wilderness area below them for dangerous riders, riders with rifles.

'You sure ain't the man to want some head money,' Booger Sam said, grinning at the game warden.

'Had I wanted the head money on you two
142

boys, I could have collected it a few days ago. I was on a high rimrock ridge, and you were under my rifle. But my job is not helping the sheriff. My job is to protect game. And besides, I know you boys have been tricked.'

Ed glanced at the man. With his belly full, the cold did not seem so intense. 'Where did this happen that you could have shot us from the saddle?'

'Over on Deer Lick Creek. I was on the rimrock.'

Ed said, 'Hard to ride the high spots all the time.'

'I was sorta suspicious of that ridge,' Booger Sam said. 'What do you want to talk to us about, Mistuh Game Warden?'

'The trouble you are in.'

Ed leaned back against a rock and sighed wearily.

'Shoot the works,' he said.

CHAPTER TEN

Faver told them all he knew. He started from the beginning, which was not too far back chronologically, and he told them about the beaver pelts that were going east out of this Greener country. Ed nodded and said he had guessed something was wrong, for a game warden did not venture out in such cold

143

weather for the sake of his health.

Suddenly Booger Sam said excitedly, 'Thet dog sled team—down in the back of the El Dorado last night—'

Faver looked from one man to the other. 'Were you boys down in town last night?'

Ed told about the visit with Sheriff Spears. Faver nodded and grinned and allowed that the sheriff must have been hopping mad, a wanted man coming into his office like that. Then Ed told about seeing the dog sled and team behind the El Dorado. 'And Downing was movin' some bales of somethin' off the sled,' he finished. 'Puttin' them in his storehouse.'

'An' this hot-headed deputy—this Fred Rome fella'—he was a-helpin' Walt Downin',' said Booger Sam.

'I went back and tried to get in that storehouse,' Ed Cotton reported. 'But they had it bolted shut, and the windows were high an' small an' had bars. An' the joint hasn't got no back door.'

'Do you figure they were bales of fur?' the game warden asked.

'They could have been,' Ed said. 'Rome sure wanted to make sure that the door was locked. He must be in cahoots with Downing, huh?'

'He must be.'

Ed said, 'Downing has been in Greener for some time, I understand. Odd, if he's tangled

144

up in this, that he hasn't been trappin' beaver before.'

'Beaver just got plentiful the last few years,' the game warden said. 'I watch one creek and they trap the other, and besides, they might be smuggling fur down from the Canucks, too.'

'Thet could be possible,' Booger Sam put in. 'Them dog sled teams seem to come in the dark.'

'Me an' Booger Sam has done some thinkin' an' talkin',' Ed said. 'And we figure now we know who has been cuttin' my fence in Black Canyon. They've cut the fence to move their dog sleds through. One time I repaired it and just the two bottom wires were cut, and that made me do some thinking. Now I know why just two were cut. With two cut, they could move their loaded sled through; the third wire was so high it never touched their load. Hell's fire man, I fenced their road off without knowin' it.'

Faver nodded. Booger Sam said nothing.

'They always went through during a blizzard or a high wind,' Ed continued. 'This washed away all tracks left by the dogs, the drive, and the sled. So I ups and blames it on Big Jim, an' all the time he swore up and down he never cut it. But me, I get bullheaded at times.'

'Well does Ah know that,' Booger Sam said seriously.

'My friend,' Ed said.

'You boys got it doped out like I have,' Curt Faver said.

'Downing wanted me to blame Big Jim for cuttin' my fence.' Ed Cotton spoke in a low voice. 'He figured me an' Big Jim—or one of Big Jim's hands—would have words that might lead to guns, and I might get killed. Which would be all to Downing's benefit, for then the fence would get ripped out.'

'And Black Canyon is about the only place that a dog team can get through, in high snow, to get into Greener,' Booger Sam said. 'Or so the Looie here tells me.'

'Looie?' Faver made it a question.

'He used to be my lieutenant in the war, suh.'

'Oh, I see.'

'Rome and Cartwright Nagle wanted to kill me that day they rode out to arrest me on that trumped-up charge of murderin' Martin Jones. I wondered at the time why they seemed so anxious to pump lead into me, but I know for sure now. They were working for Downing.'

'Maybe Big Jim is in cahoots with Downin'?' Booger Sam put the question out into the cold arctic air.

But Curt Faver shook his head. 'Big Jim is no thief. No, Downing and his hands are in this and are not helped by the Triangle Diamond.'

Ed said, 'Downing offered to go my bail so he could get me out of jail and kill me from the brush. I wonder if he killed Martin Jones, too, to lay the blame on me. But that is purty cold-blooded. He must've had another reason for killin' Jones, if he did really kill him.'

'He killed him. Either he or one of his hands,' Faver stated positively.

Ed Cotton studied the game warden's thin face. 'You seem certain of that,' he said. 'What makes you so positive, Faver?'

'Jones worked for Downing.'

'You don't say,' ejaculated Booger Sam. 'Say, Looie, this plot is gettin' thick, huh?'

Ed spoke to Curt Faver. 'Go on,' he said. 'Explain.'

The explanation was simple. Jones had been trapping beaver on Big Jim Wilford's Triangle Diamond range. There were a number of sloughs on the big spread, and these all held beaver. Also, there were creeks to the north, and these also were breeding grounds for the wide-tailed animal.

'Downing has trappers out. I can't patrol this whole area—it's bigger than most eastern states. But some of those creeks have little if any beaver left, men.'

'But where does Jones come into this, outside of drawing two pay checks—one from Big Jim and one from Walt Downing?' Ed was the one who asked this question.

'From here on, I have to go on guesswork,'

147

Faver said slowly. 'But I think Jones wanted a bigger cut from Downing, and they must have argued about it. Jones was drunk the night he tangled with you in the El Dorado, Ed. That night—maybe you didn't know it until now—Jones hit Downing for around five thousand in a poker game, in the back room of Downing's saloon. Downing wanted that money back. He wanted to get Jones out of circulation.'

'So him or Rome—or some other lowdown devil Downing has hired—has Jones ambushed and puts the blame on me, all on account of that fistfight I had with Jones. Talk about coincidence, that sure was a case of it.'

'I figure Downing killed him himself, because he wouldn't want anybody else to know who downed Martin Jones. But my figures might not add up, fellows, although they do sound logical to me.'

'Me, too,' Booger Sam said.

Ed played with some snow, letting it fall through his mittened hand. He was frowning.

'Then if Downing killed Jones, Downing cut my fence to make it look like Jones did it, huh?' He did not wait for an answer; none was necessary. 'Then he looks for Big Jim to sign a warrant against me, which Big Jim did. Rome and Nagle come to serve the warrant and to kill me. Man alive, Booger, I sure was lucky you came along, or they would have murdered me in that cell!'

'For once I did somethin' right, Looie.'

'And then Downing offered to go your bail, to get you out so he could kill you—and lay the blame on Big Jim Wilford,' the game warden explained. 'You see, there are still some beaver on Big Jim's spread, and Downing could trap them easier. Nobody would be much interested in beaver—with Big Jim in jail, and all that talk going around. Nobody would have time to ride range or think about beaver.'

'I don't follow you on that,' Ed Cotton said.

The game warden gestured impatiently. 'You see, Ed, those remaining beaver—well, they are located pretty close to the Triangle Diamond ranch house.'

'Oh,' Ed replied.

'I figured I'd make contact with you, and the three of us could work together,' the game warden said. 'That helper of mine is no good to me, so I made him stay home. He'd freeze to death, dumb as he is.'

'We might just as well camp here,' Ed said. 'Good place. We can see the range below us and nobody can get higher than us, like you did to me an' Booger that day, Curt.'

But Faver shook his head.

'No rest for the wicked . . . and a game warden. I'll scout Rocky Gorge. You two boys scout Black Canyon. To get their furs to

149

the railroad, they have to go through either of those two canyons with their dog sleds and teams.'

'They must store their furs in Downing's warehouse,' Ed Cotton put in. 'Then when they get enough for a shipment they pull sleds to the railhead, and ship out from there?'

'So I figure.' Faver killed the pot of coffee. 'We throw snow on this fire to kill it.' He scooped snow in his mittened hands. It hit the fire, sputtered, and the fire was dead. He got to his feet and slipped into his pack. 'I got a hunch Rocky Gorge is full of snow. But to get off the plateau, they have to take a canyon down to the level land. Rocky Gorge might be snowed shut.'

'That bein' the case,' Booger Sam said, 'they'd have to go down Black Canyon, huh?'

'That's the deal,' Ed Cotton said.

Faver said, 'And you ran your fence right across their trail, Ed.'

Ed grinned wryly. 'Now he tells me,' he said.

Faver said, 'So long,' and moved away, snowshoes padding the snow. He looked weary and his shoulders were bent, but still there was a tough resilience in the man. He carried his rifle in one hand.

Booger Sam said, 'Us'n for Black Canyon, eh?'

'So it would appear,' Ed said.

They took to the brush twice to escape

150

being seen by riders moving below them. But the riders turned out to be Triangle Diamond hands out hazing strays back toward the feed lots. Sometimes the cattle strayed with the storm, seeking grass on the ridges where the wind had whipped away the snow. They were weak, and if they were out too long they would die; therefore riders were out to turn them back toward the Wilford feed yards.

'You northern boys sure has a tough winter.' Booger Sam sat his horse and watched the riders hazing the bony stock. 'If this hangs on long, there's gonna be a heap of winter-killed cows on this range, Lieutenant.'

Ed Cotton watched the riders through narrowed eyes. His eyes were bloodshot because of the dazzling sun on the white snow.

'We had a summer without rain, Booger. The cricks almost went dry. Would have dried up, if'n the beavers hadn't been busy buildin' dams to hold back the water. Them beaver sure are handy to a cowman come a drought. Then along last September, there come some hard rains. They were too late to help the grass much—but they did refill the cricks and waterholes.'

Booger Sam spoke in a low voice. 'Wonder if'n Big Jim Wilford ain't ordered his riders to keep their noses out of our trouble.'

'Why would he do that?'

'Well, first place I think he saw he was on

151

the wrong side. Second place, thet purty daughter of his is kinda gone on a long-legged cowpoke named Ed Cotton.'

Ed rubbed his whiskery jaw. 'You got a vivid imagination.'

'Why do you say that?'

'She's the daughter of a cattle king, you fool, and I'm jes' a misguided nester, squattin' on land claimed by her pappy.'

'This thing called love is a queer thing.'

'How do you know?'

This seemed to stump the Negro. He grinned widely and said nothing. They watched the Triangle Diamond riders chouse the cows over the ridge and disappear when the hill came up behind them. They rode forward. They hung to the ridges for two reasons. One was that there was less snow here—the wind had swept it off the rocky gravel terrain. Then, also, they could see clearly below them.

Within an hour they came to Black Canyon, so named because of its dark igneous rock walls—walls now covered with snow.

Scrub pine and scrub cedar clung to the steep walls, rearing their evergreen heads out of the snow. To get to the railroad there were just two passes through this area, and Black Canyon was one of them. Rocky Gorge, about five miles to the east, was the other. They were about a mile above Ed's drift fence. The bottom of the canyon spread out as it ran to meet the plains below. The canyon was passable; a sled and dogs could move along its bottom. They scouted down to the fence, taking their time, sometimes walking and leading their broncs. They did not traverse the bottom of the canyon. Here the snow was unbroken, for it had drifted in—it lay serene and cold and white. They moved along the lip of the canyon. They encountered boulders, half-covered by snow, and then they were back of the drift fence. Ed put the glasses on the wires, but could not see clearly whether they were intact or whether they were down.

'I want to look at that fence,' he told his partner.

'Might be risky. They might have men ridin' patrol on the bobwire, Looie.'

Ed shook his head. 'I got to make sure.'

'I'll wait for you here . . . an' stand guard with my rifle.'

Ed went down the side of the canyon on foot, rifle in hand. Once he slipped in the snow and got snow in the breech of his Winchester. He squatted among some boulders and cleaned out the mechanism, for he could not afford to let the snow melt under the heat of his mitten and freeze in the ejector. To do so would be to commit suicide, had he need to use the rifle suddenly. He had to be ready for any emergency.

Finally he came to the drift fence. The fence was not cut. The wires were tauter than ever, pulled even tighter by the intense cold. When he had patched the fence, he had used wire stretchers. Now it would take a pair of wire-cutting pliers to cut the wires. He laboriously climbed the slope, working his way back to where Booger Sam waited with his rifle. When he reached the Negro, he was puffing like a bay steer that had been run hard on a hot August day.

'Nobody's cut them yet, Booger.'

'Wonder how many sleds full they pull through at one time? Maybe just one sled, huh?'

'We'll ask Faver . . . when we see him again.'

There was nothing to do but go back to Faver's rimrock camp. When they rode in, Faver was boiling coffee. He looked up, and a small smile pulled at his chapped lips.

'Rocky Gorge is completely snowed in, men. Snow from one lip of the gorge to the other—wind whipped it in. Only a bird could go down it, and he would have to fly.'

Ed dismounted, his bones saddle-weary. 'Then they have to move down Black Canyon,' he said.

'No other way down off the plateau to the railhead,' the game warden said. 'Light and get outside of some java.'

Booger Sam stretched. His sockets creaked. 'Gettin' ol',' he mumbled. 'Wonder when they will move.'

154

Faver said, 'We don't know.'

Ed poured coffee into himself, drinking from the pot. 'Only thing we can do,' he said, 'is keep a guard, along where the fence is. And the night is gonna be cold, too.'

They spent the rest of the short day in the rocks. Ed sat with his back against a boulder and watched the range below with his field glasses. He saw a rider leave the Triangle Diamond, about five miles away, and ride to his homestead. The rider passed about half-mile from their camp. The glasses showed that it was not Connie. She was sending over a cowpuncher to feed his chickens, slop his hogs, and dole out hay to his stock and feed his dog. What would he have done without Connie?

Nightfall found the three of them stationed along the base of Black Canyon, directly below the fence. Their plan was to let the fur smugglers cut the fence; then they would challenge them. Ed was stationed on the bottom of the canyon, there behind some boulders; Booger Sam took the west side of the canyon, squatting in the boulders along the steep back. Game Warden Curt Faver took the east bank, hiding in some brush.

The night was dazzling bright, for the moon was sharp on the fresh white·snow. And the night was bitterly cold. A man could not stand still long. He had to move around or freeze to death. Ed had many ideas. One was that they should openly raid the warehouse behind the El Dorado. Go in with their guns, line up Rome and Downing, make them take down the padlock. But this plan, logic told him, was not a good one—a thief has to be caught in the act. Even if the beaver pelts found in the warehouse—and he was sure there were beaver furs there—did not have the official stamp of the state and Uncle Sam on the flesh side of the pelt, they would still have to pin the ownership of these furs on Downing and to Rome. And this might be difficult.

No, the thing to do—the only thing to do—was to intercept the sleds carrying the illegitimate furs to the railhead.

But no furs were moved that night.

Dawn came with cold sullenness. There was no snow falling, but the thermometer was low in the bulb. Ed and Booger Sam returned to the rimrock hideaway. It was the best place to hide; there was food there. Curt Fayer went to Greener.

'Going to scout around, men.'

Ed disliked seeing the game warden go, for some reason. From the high butte, he and his partner watched the game warden trek across the wilderness of snow until he became a small dot and distance claimed him.

'Sure as heck a cold day,' Booger Sam said. 'Let's make some coffee.'

'Best idea any of us has had for a long

156

time.'

CHAPTER ELEVEN

Walt Downing played a card and squinted at his hand over his cigar. It was nice and warm in the poker room of the El Dorado, for the heater was cherry red. He was playing whist with the old hostler.

'They done stole two hosses out of my barn,' the old man said. He was, as usual, half drunk. He didn't have to drink more than one or two drinks to get drunk, because his body was so full of alcohol. 'Big Jim Wilford ate me out, lettin' them hosses be stole from under my nose.'

'You've told me that about ten times,' Downing grumbled. 'Your play, ol' man. Can you see your cards?'

'Is you implyin' that I'm drunk?' The old man pretended to be hurt.

Downing moved his cigar to the other corner of his mouth. 'You're not drunk,' he said. 'You're pickled.'

The old man laboriously made his play. 'Big Jim never swore out a warrant for them two hoss thieves, and that sure got me su'prised.'

Walt Downing said nothing in reply. The whole country considered it odd that Big Jim, who boasted he was death to a horse thief, had not taken the trail of Booger Sam and Ed Cotton. But everybody realized that this was because of Connie. She had kept her father from swearing out a warrant. Was she in love with this Cotton gent?

Downing was puzzled. Everything he had done seemed to have gone wrong. First he had expected Nagle and Rome to kill Ed Cotton. Then the drift fence could have been jerked out, and his dog sleds would have gone down Black Canyon without anybody knowing a vehicle had moved through the fence. But they had not killed Cotton, because Big Jim Wilford had butted in. And Nagle was dead now, six feet under the snow. It was a strange world.

'Play, dang you,' he told his partner.

'You sound rough today, Walt.'

Downing smiled around his cigar. 'I am rough.'

They finished the game—which seemed endless to Downing—and they went into the main part of the El Dorado. Business was slack because of the cold snap. Two Triangle Diamond boys had drifted into town, unbeknown to Big Jim, who had sent them out on the range to turn back drifting cattle. They were sitting around the stove with a few of the town loafers. The saloon was cold except when a man sat beside the stove. Downing said to the bartender, 'Give the ol' man a drink, because he beat me,' and waved generously with his cigar. Impatience was in him, but he held it with stern reins. His beefy face did not show his irritation. He was alone at the end of the bar close to the stove when Deputy Sheriff Fred Rome came in, his face ruddy from the cold. Rome stamped snow from his overshoes and unwrapped his muffler.

'Cold,' he said.

'We all know that,' Downing said shortly.

Rome bought a cigar and bit off the end.

One of the cowpunchers asked, 'You done caught them two criminals yet, Fred?'

Rome looked at the man in the back bar mirror. His match was to his cigar. He got the impression that the cowpoke was joshing him, but he was not sure. For a moment he felt anger, and then he shoved this to one side.

'Not yet, Nixon.'

A loafer said, 'Somebody claims he sighted them way over on South Crick, driftin' south. Yesterday mawnin', that was.'

Downing listened, turned his glass of whisky on the bar, and said nothing. A man could learn a lot by keeping his mouth shut and his ears nailed back.

'They must've left the country,' Rome said. 'We've done looked good, but it's a big range.'

'With a heap of snow on it,' another man said. 'Man an' boy, I've bin in the kentry for

159

forty-three years, but I never seen snow this deep before. So darn deep Big Jim had trouble gettin' a team an' a bobsled into town. Snow so deep in the cuts he had to take to the side hills.'

'Wonder if they done lit out of the kentry?' another asked.

'They'd show sense if they did,' a cowpuncher said. 'But Big Jim—he never moved against them—even if they did steal two fresh hosses of his. I think they stole them hosses an' then lit out for the south while they was astraddle good strong hossflesh.'

And so the talk went back and forth, and it was all based on conjecture. Downing finished his drink and returned to his office, and soon Rome called, 'A game, Walt?'

'Maybe.'

Rome came into the office. He said, 'Spears is talkin' about pullin' the men off the trail.'

'Thinks they've skipped the country, huh?'

'I don't know about that. But Big Jim is ridin' him hard, claimin' a big payroll is a waste of money. And Big Jim is a county commissioner.'

Downing nodded and relit his cigar. 'They might have pulled out, at that, though it don't seem logical that Cotton would leave his spread. But nobody has seen anything of them for some time now.'

'Wonder where Faver is?'

'Nobody has seen him, either.'

Rome walked to the stove and warmed his hands. Downing stood and looked at his desk. Idly he fingered an envelope. He seemed thoughtful. Finally he said, 'I'm going to take a ride.'

'Want me to go with you?'

'No. Won't look good, you hangin' close to me so much.'

'Yeah, reckon that is right.'

Downing pulled on a pair of angora chaps. He put on overshoes and a coat, and over this he put his sheep-skin coat. He wore mittens, and he picked up his rifle, and Rome said, 'When do we drive the furs through?'

Downing stopped. 'That trapper on Down Crick has to take in his catch before we move.'

'When will he be in?'

'Tonight, I hope. He's laid back some the last few days. Even pulled up his traps, I fear.'

'Faver?'

'Faver is on to something,' Downing said, and went outside. Rome went to the main part of the saloon. He was killing a fast drink when Curt Faver came in. Faver had gone home, and he was clean-shaven; he was full of breakfast and hot coffee. This did much to hide his look of weariness.

Faver said, 'Cold weather.'

Rome felt rebellion rise in him. Everybody

161

talked about the weather! He said, 'Drink, Curt?'

'One.'

Rome ordered and considered Faver. The man was on the trail. He was sure of that. What did Faver know? How nice and handy it would be if a man could read the thoughts of another!

They drank, and Faver bought a drink—a single drink—and this went to Rome. They talked about things of little if any importance. Faver left the saloon, saying, 'Got to get to my office and do my book work.'

'You got an assistant now, so why doesn't he do it?'

Faver stopped at the door and showed his tired smile. 'I wonder why the devil they sent me a helper?' He was fishing for something.

But the bait was no good, for Rome said, 'Can't tell about women, or the big shots in the gover'ment.'

Faver stepped out on the overshoe-pounded snow. He had gained nothing by dropping in on the El Dorado. But a man had to follow his hunches. He decided to go home and get some sleep, for there was a night ahead. A cold night, in a canyon. He had reached the end of the street when Walt Downing rode out of the alley. Downing rode a grey horse, and the horse was big and so was the rider.

Faver said, 'Cold weather to ride in, Walt.'

162

Downing looked at him over his cigar. 'Ought to break sometime,' he said. 'Sure, it has to break.'

'Sometime,' Faver said.

They said no more, and Faver went to his home and Downing rode to the Cotton farm. Downing was restless, and he found company in the wilderness, for it seemed to brood and hold in its snow-filled surface a vagueness and a hint of peace. Downing did not know why he thought that way. He grew more peaceful, and some of the push died in his big body. Everything had gone wrong. From the start, it had all gone haywire. Well, one more big shipment of fur, and it would be the last. He'd have it made . . . for this year. Faver was out on the trail too much. When the trapper on Down Creek came in with his beaver, then the sleds would move out. Two sleds, carrying thousands of dollars worth of beaver pelts.

He came to Ed Cotton's fence and he rode along it, and the ironical thought came that the strands of barbed wire—shiny and sharp—were the cause of it all.

When he came to Cotton's farm, there was only one guard stationed. He was in the house, and he came out with his rifle, and he recognized Downing and said, 'Howdy, Walt.'

'No sign of the criminals?'

'Nary a trace, Walt.'

163

Downing said, 'Any coffee?'

'Sure.'

Downing dismounted and went into the cabin and drank three quick cups of coffee. He and the guard spoke little. The guard was convinced that Cotton and the coloured man had jumped the country. Downing got up into his saddle again and rode on. He scanned the country and he talked with two Triangle Diamond riders who were hazing back strays, and they also had seen no sign of the wanted men. Downing rode to the Triangle Diamond.

Snow was draped over the buildings. Cattle stood in the feed yards, and occasionally one of them bawled in protest against the storm gods and his empty belly. Downing gave the hay piles a glance and thought, He's getting low on hay.

Big Jim was shoeing a saddle horse in front of the blacksmith shop. He was hammering down the nails in the off-front hoof when Downing rode in. Big Jim glanced up and said, 'Hello, Downing.'

He did not ask Downing to come down. Downing was quick to notice this, and he held his scowl back.

'Cold weather, Jim.'

'It'll break.'

Downing took his overshoes out of his stirrups and stretched his legs. 'No sign of Cotton,' he said.

164

Big Jim hammered a nail in and clinched it. The horse fiddled a little, and Big Jim swore at him.

'You can pull out that drift fence now,' Downing said. 'Greener's only farmer has been run off, and the Triangle Diamond has won its point.'

'We don't need no nesters.'

'No place for barbed wire on this range.'

Connie Wilford came out of the barn, where she had been feeding her saddle horse. The cold touched her cheeks and made high colour there. Even with her long overcoat, she looked feminine. She said hello and went on to the house. Downing thought. This outfit is giving me the brush-off. He had never got along well with Big Jim. There had always been animosity between them. Downing knew some of it was caused by the fact that he did not work for his money—he was, in Big Jim's eyes, a parasite. Big Jim had many times expressed his dislike for men who worked indoors.

Downing realised he could accomplish nothing on this ranch. He had wanted to talk to Big Jim about Ed Cotton and Booger Sam, to find out the man's opinion. But Big Jim evidently was not in a talking mood. He was like the rest of the men on this range.

Downing turned his horse. 'So long, Wilford.'

'So long.'

165

There was no more said. Downing reined the grey around and rode away. The land lifted and the land was white, broken only by the tips of igneous boulders and pine and spruce and the gaunt limbs of the leafless cottonwoods that were sleeping until the magic of spring again came to this land. The land rolled and the land slept, and the land told nothing.

Downing rode toward Down Creek. The sloughs below the Triangle Diamond were frozen shut and snow covered the ice; under that ice and that snow were beavers. The richest colony was in his slough, and he could not touch it because of its proximity to the Triangle Diamond ranch-house.

His mind went to the subject dearest to him. He had cleared around thirty thousand off beaver pelts and this next shipment would pay around two thousand, if not more. He had had to cut in Rome and the trappers, but after this shipment the trappers would drift. There were only two of them, and a thousand for each was big money. Nagle had taken himself out of this by a bullet. He had gained when Nagle had been killed. Rome was the sore spot—he was not too strong. So he decided to eliminate Rome. On the way back from the railhead, Rome would die. There was always a crevice, and the snow would claim him for its own.

People would figure that Rome had run

into Cotton and the Negro, and had been killed in a gunfight. Things were working out all right, at that.

The Down Creek trapper had a lean-to in the high brush. He was not in the lean-to when Downing rode up, and Downing was ready to ride away when the man came out of the brush.

'Playin' it close,' he said. 'Howdy, Walt.'

Downing nodded. 'Ready to move fur, Jim?'

'She's all trapped out. I had to lay low for a day or so.'

'Faver?'

'Yes, the warden. I pulled out my traps. He scouted the crick. But no traps were set.'

'Good.'

'I'll move my fur in tonight, around midnight. Got a good catch.' A sled dog was with the man. 'I'll pack some, and Smoky can pull in the toboggan.'

'Come in behind the spread.'

'Same as usual.'

Downing said, 'Around midnight,' and turned his horse. 'Then you get your pay and get out of this country.'

'Just what I want to do.'

'You're the last,' Downing said. 'Ike went two days ago. Got his cut and left.'

'Gold.'

'If you want it, gold it will be.'

'I don't like them paper bills.'

Downing was in no mood to discuss the relative merits of gold and paper as payment.

'Gold,' he repeated, and left.

He loped across the places where the snow was not too deep, and where the snow was deep the grey went at a walk. He had decided to eliminate the other trapper. He had outlived his usefulness. He had told Jim that Ike had left the country. This was not true.

But soon he would leave the country . . . for good.

Downing killed the man within two hours. He shot him from concealment in the brush and he left him in the snow beside his lean-to. The man had a few beaver pelts on the dryers, but Downing left them there. He had used the man, and the man was dead, and Downing looked at the body without emotion. He rode on, and the wind came in and hid his horse's tracks. The wind piled the snow against the dead man—the man who would never know who had killed him.

Downing rode toward Greener.

From the high butte, two sets of eyes watched him. One set belonged to a Negro—a wide man still marked by the savagery of war. The other set belonged to the Negro's partner.

Ed said, 'That looks like Walt Downing.' He handed the glasses to Booger Sam. Booger Sam looked and said, 'Can't tell. Only saw him once or twice. Could be anybody.'

'Downing, I think.'

The Negro sat down, back against the boulder. He was cold to the bone. 'Wish Faver would come back,' he said.

'He might bring some news.'

But Curt Faver did not come that day. The day ran its slow length and the world was cold.

'Wonder if I'll ever git warm again?' Booger Sam asked himself. He was pacing back and forth.

Ed smiled. 'You'll warm up in a hurry if they hang you for horse-stealing.'

Booger Sam stopped and looked at him.

'What a cheerful cuss you is, Looie!'

Ed Cotton got to his feet. 'Time we took up stations in that canyon,' he told his companion. 'Sure hope they move fur tonight.'

'Where the heck is the game warden?'

CHAPTER TWELVE

The night was clear and cold. No snow fell, and the moon was in a sky without clouds. The moon was very, very bright. You could see the hills and you could see the dark spots on the rimrock where the boulders protruded through the snow. You could see the dark area of pine and spruce on the sides of Black

Canyon. The moon hung in the sky and said nothing.

Walt Downing was impatient. He was waiting for the trapper to come in; the man came in about midnight. Downing paced the floor of his office. He was ready for the trail, complete with overshoes and mittens and long sheepskin coat. Fred Rome lay on the bunk and watched the big man. Rome had slow and speculative eyes, and Rome said nothing. Downing walked and walked, because walking made the devils lie down for a while.

'He should be here,' Downing said.

Rome said, 'The dogs and sleds are ready. But this bright moonlight—I don't like it so bright, Walt.'

'Nobody will see us leave town.'

'Faver might be on the prowl.'

'I doubt that.' Downing stopped and listened. 'Somebody out in the alley now, Fred.'

'I never heard nothin'.'

'Your ears are bad.'

Rome climbed to his feet. The office stove was dead; the room was frigid. Downing went to the door. Rome followed. Downing was right; the trapper was there. He had a pack on his back, the moose-hide straps running over his shoulders. He had a dog hitched to a toboggan and a stack of pelts on the flat sled. He said, 'I got here, Walt.'

'Get that rig into the storehouse, and make

170

it snappy.'

'I'll open the door,' Rome said.

Rome unlocked the door, and the dog and trapper went into the storehouse, with Walt Downing following and Rome walking ahead. Here a lantern was lit. There too were two teams of huskies, hitched to low sleds. The sleds were loaded; the dogs were ready for the trail. One smelled the strange dog and he growled, and the sound was low and rumbling. Some stood and others lay down. They were wild creatures and the wolf strain was strong in them. Downing did not keep them in town—he had them penned out at his ranch. Few people knew he had the dogs. People did not know he owned them; those who knew figured they belonged to his two trappers.

Downing said, 'You can transfer your furs to a sled, Jim, or run through with us the way things are—carrying your furs on that toboggan.'

'I'm not runnin' fur through,' the trapper said.

Downing nodded and said, 'Okay, okay, okay. Put your bundle on this first sled and tie it down. You'd best run your furs through with us, though. You ain't got no call to stay here in town.'

'I want to stick around Greener for a while. I know a woman in the hotel and—'

Downing said, 'You come with us. Woman

171

or no woman, you leave Greener—you pull out of this country. Whisky loosens your tongue, and you might talk. Jim, don't cause me no trouble.'

'This woman—'

'She's already got another man, you fool. Martin Jamison is shining up to her. You were gone too long in the wilderness. Now you're going with us, or no pay. Savvy that? No pay unless you go.'

'You'll pay me at the railhead?'

'Only then,' said Walt Downing. 'Only then . . .'

The man cursed the woman. He sobered and said, 'I'll go with you.' He looked at the huskies and the sleds. 'We should scout ahead, to make sure nobody sees us leave.'

'Your job—and Rome's job.'

'Come along, Fred,' the trapper said.

They left the building. Downing was alone with the dogs. The lantern, hanging from a spike in a post, showed its dim yellow light. It reflected off the dark sheen of the dogs' fur. Downing moved over and went to his knees and petted the lead dog of the first sled. The dog licked Downing's face. Downing put his arms around the great shaggy neck and lowered his head against that of the dog, and for a moment a great loneliness came over the man. He had no wife, he had no child, he had no kin. He had only himself and his driving desires. He straightened and said, 'Good dog,

Smoky,' and was himself again. He waited, and ten minutes ran by. Soon Rome and the trapper returned.

Rome said, 'The whole town is asleep. But I do wish it was snowing, Walt. Snow would hide us. First time we ever pulled out a load in the moonlight. All the other times, it was snowing hard.'

'First time for everything' Downing grunted. 'Did you scout Faver's house?'

'We did,' Rome said. He added, 'All dark.'

'His office, too?'

'That was dark, too.'

'Good.'

'We get movin'?' the trapper asked.

'Move the dogs,' Downing ordered.

Rome swung the door open and the dogs went to work. They had thrown snow into the storehouse, and this made the sleds easy to move. They whined and leaped against their traces, hungry for snow and the trail. They bunched and dug into the snow; the sleds slipped forward. They were low, and when the snow got too deep their runners did not guide the sled; they rode the snow like toboggans. Downing headed them. He had snowshoes strapped on his back and he carried his rifle. Rome came behind the first sled, trotting along, and the trapper followed the last sled. They moved into the alley, and here the sleds were easy to move, for the snow was pounded down and icy. They swung down the alley and were out of town in a minute or two.

Greener slept. There were no lights. Somewhere in the distance a wolf howled, and the dogs wanted to answer, but they were working and could not yelp. Downing headed them out on to the packed road. Bob-sleds and horses had tramped the trail hard. They left Greener behind them and the earth held them; the snow-filled distance made them prisoners. They moved through this silence, and they were silent and dark in the moonlight. They went at a trot, with Downing leading. Sweat came out and warmed him. He glanced back and saw that Rome had hitched a ride on the back of the sled. He growled, 'None of that, for it drags the dogs down, and we have a long pull.' Rome dropped off the sled and trotted, but he was angry.

Downing glanced back at the trapper. The man was trotting, not hitching a ride. Downing stood for a moment, and the lead sled went by, and Downing was trotting beside Rome. Downing said, 'Nobody saw us leave.'

'Nobody saw us,' Rome repeated.

But Downing was wrong. A man had seen them leave Greener. He had been hidden between two buildings in the darkness. Now he trailed them, and he carried his rifle.

Booger Sam's hands were cold. He swung his arms to restore circulation and the moonlight washed across his big body. He said. 'Looie, how many days has we been in this snow?'

'Too many,' Ed Cotton said.

'Must be about four years, huh?'

'I'd say closer to ten,' Ed joked.

'Looie, what say when this is over—if it ever gets over—we join the army again?'

'Now you are delirious,' Ed said.

The Negro dropped his arms. 'I kinda liked the army in one way,' he said. 'We always had warm barracks.'

'Forget it, Booger, please.'

'You never did like the armed forces?'

'Oh, forget it.'

'You sound kinda mad.'

'I am mad,' Ed said.

'I'm kinda mad too. But I'm mad at myself.'

Ed grinned. 'Reckon I'm mad at myself, too.'

They were stationed on the east side of Black Canyon. They were about three hundred feet below the drift fence. A coyote talked in the distance, and from another ridge there came his answer. Coyotes were sleek and glossy, for they lived off winter-killed cows. These sounds died, and there was only the sibilant whisper of the wilderness and its snow—the silent murmur of great spaces. They were about thirty feet up the canyon wall, behind some granite boulders. They had tramped the snow flat as they had walked to keep warm. Ed figured it was close to midnight; they had been in this spot for about six hours. His mind darted here and there and he thought of many things. The men they were waiting for would have to go down this canyon to get to the level ground. That much was certain. But when would they come? This was not certain.

'Faver,' Ed said. 'Wonder where he is?'

'He'd come to warn us if they aimed to move furs, wouldn't he?'

'I guess so.'

'I'm cold.'

Ed said, 'Don't repeat yourself so much. When this is over we'll sit beside the fire and warm up for the rest of the winter.'

'Big Jim might want to hang us as hoss thieves.'

'You're a cheerful cuss.'

They talked some more, and time went on, and the wilderness held its secret. Ed said, 'I'll scout ahead,' and Booger Sam said, 'I'll go with you.'

'Why?'

'I ain't got no answer to thet.'

Ed said, 'Somebody has to watch. They might sneak by us, you know. I'll be back right pronto.'

Booger Sam said nothing. Ed climbed the slope to where they had cached their horses. The horses were in a bunch of fir trees. They were cold and they were getting gaunt from lack of hay and oats. Ed petted one of them for a moment, running his mittened hand over the bronc's bony nose. The horse pushed against him, and Ed pulled back. He scouted toward Greener. But the night showed nothing, no dark spots moved across it, and he returned to where Booger Sam waited with raw impatience.

'See anythin', Looie?'

'Only the snow—and more snow.'

Booger Sam looked at the moon. 'Wonder if for sure there is a man up there?' he asked.

'His name,' said Ed, 'is Booger Sam.'

'Wonder where Faver is?'

'I don't know.'

At this moment Curt Faver was trailing the two dog sleds. He had swung in behind them. He travelled about a quarter-mile behind them, hoping he was hidden. Wherever possible, he moved along the ridges where the evergreens hid him. He only hoped that Ed Cotton and the Negro were stationed in Black Canyon. If they were not there, then he would follow the pelts to the railhead; he would get help and then make his arrests. Anyway, he would have Downing and Rome with the goods.

They came to the point where the Canyon

177

started its downward dip. The two dog sleds and the men left the high ground and were lost from view in the fall of the Canyon. Faver moved forward now at a faster pace, and sweat was on his body—it made his woollen underwear stick to his muscles. He went at an even faster pace. He thought, from here to the drift fence is about four miles.

He thought, I wonder if Booger and Ed are stationed.

He moved forward, and moonlight glistened off the barrel of his cold Winchester rifle.

CHAPTER THIRTEEN

Booger Sam was the first to hear the approaching dog teams. He said, 'I hear somethin',' and Ed Cotton stopped his endless pacing. Something in the Negro's voice drove a chill into muscles already cold.

Ed listened, but heard nothing.

Ed said, 'Your imagination—' Then he stopped speaking. 'I hear it, too, Booger.'

The Negro had moved out around the rocks to where he could look up the Canyon. He was a solid man, there in the moonlight. Ed moved out beside him, and they looked toward the north.

'Somethin' is comin', Looie.'

'You don't suppose it's them?'

'We should have some luck sometime.'

'I can't see anything.'

'Wait awhile.'

'Might have been cattle, driftin' toward the fence. They used to water below here.'

'I even smell somethin', Looie.'

Ed said, 'There's somethin' up there—movin' toward us. Man alive, Booger, that's a dog team.'

'Two of them, looks to me like.'

'Two of them,' Ed confirmed.

They were silent for a moment. Now they could see the dog teams and sleds; they could even see the men, although they were mere dark pencils against the snow—pencils that moved.

'Three men,' Booger Sam said.

'And only two of us,' Ed said.

'Our usual luck, Looie.'

Ed said, 'You take your station at the far end of the boulders, and I'll move to the other end. Let them get through the fence—let them cut the fence—and then I'll challenge them.'

Booger Sam looked at him, and his eyes were sad. 'Reminds me of San Juan a little.'

'Only no snow there,' Ed reminded him.

Booger Sam grabbed Ed's forearm. He shook him and said, 'Good luck, Looie. Good luck.'

'Same to you.'

The teams were now a quarter-mile or less away. Ed heard Booger Sam's overshoes crunch away, and then this sound was lost as the man moved beyond hearing range. Ed glanced around, and Booger Sam was gone, the boulders hiding him. He looked at the men and the dogs and the sleds. They came to the drift fence and the lead dog stopped, and the entire procession came to a halt.

A voice said, 'I'll cut his blasted fence.'

Ed thought, That voice belongs to Walt Downing. Luck was with them. They would get the king-pin.

'Cut it pronto, and let us get going again.'

Ed did not know that voice.

He watched as Downing got a pair of fence pliers off the sled and then went to the fence. Ed heard the wires part. They were taut with the cold; they snapped like .22 reports. One by one they went into two parts. Then Downing put the pliers in his overcoat pocket.

'We'll move on,' he said.

The teams moved, and the men trotted. Ed dropped his mitten to the snow so his hand would be free on the trigger. He waited, and he thought once he saw a movement in the brush, along the canyon's wall. But the moonlight was fickle and he paid no attention, blaming the image on shifting shadows. His throat was dry. He hoped he would live through the gunfight ahead. He

180

knew Downing and his men would fight.

Then the sleds were below him, not more than thirty feet away, and his voice cut through the cold stillness.

'Stop them dogs, and throw away your weapons!'

★   ★   ★

There was a moment then when the cold world seemed suspended in nothingness. Downing stopped in his tracks, and the dogs also stopped, the sleds running against the hind legs of the rear dogs. Now Ed could recognise Fred Rome, too, and he thought, We got them both, and that is good. And then the voice of Booger Sam, about ten feet away, cut across the suspense, breaking it and shattering it like a hammer smashing into a fragile vase.

'Throw away your guns, men!'

Fred Rome was the one who hollered, 'It's them two—it's Cotton and the black man! They never left the country—they've set a trap for us!'

The third man, the one at the rear, hollered, 'I'm makin' tracks. Don't shoot me, Cotton!'

He turned to run, but he got only a few paces. That was because Downing had gone to one knee, and he had shot the man through the back. The man went down, stumbling as he fell, and Downing turned the rifle on Ed Cotton. And Downing hollered, 'Kill the devils, Rome!'

Ed went to his knees, thereby making a smaller target. Downing had moved suddenly, and Downing was so fast he got in the first shot. Ed remembered later that Downing's bullet had smashed against the boulder at his right. It was later that he remembered this, because all was lost now in the rapid fire of battle.

He remembered, too, that Booger Sam had hollered something, and later he realised this had been the old battle-cry—the cry that had accompanied them up bloody San Juan Hill in the war now gone but never to be forgotten. Ed remembered his rifle leaping back against the overcoat padding of his shoulder, and he remembered he had missed. And Downing shot again.

This time Downing's bullet did not hit the rock. It went upward at a 45-degree angle toward the moon. Ed had shot at the same time and he had hit Downing in the chest. Downing got to his feet, screaming words without meaning, and he dropped his rifle into the snow. The dogs stampeded, and then a sled overturned, holding them in a wicked ugly pack—a snarling pack of half-wild canines. Ed turned his rifle on Rome, but Rome was already down. He was hollering for help, and his words were hoarse and harsh.

'I got Rome,' Booger Sam said.

Ed said, 'I remember him shootin'. Did he get you?'

Booger Sam limped down the slope. 'Through the meat of my leg,' he said. 'Between my knee and my ankle. I can feel the blood.'

Suddenly the Negro sat down. He had a foolish grin on his wide face.

'My leg—he got tired.'

'You think the bone is broke?'

Ed thought, My voice sure is shaky.

'Nah, it ain't busted. Just the meat. Check on them devils, Ed. It took a long time to build up, but it was over in a heck of a hurry.'

Ed said, 'Here comes somebody.'

A man hollered, 'Curt Faver coming in,' and Booger Sam grinned and hollered back, 'You're late, as usual.'

Ed was standing over Walt Downing. He saw the man's face, and he said, 'He looks dead to me,' and he moved over to where Rome was on his knees, whimpering like a sick puppy.

'You hurt bad, Rome?'

'My shoulder—'

Ed did not let him finish. He used his rifle like a bayonet, only the barrel did not hit Rome's head—he hit him with the butt plate. Rome said nothing. He went on his face into the snow, knocked cold. Ed looked at Curt

183

Faver, and afterwards Faver said his face looked like the face of a man who had come out of purgatory.

'We got them, Faver.'

Faver tried to talk. He wet his lips.

But no words came.

★   ★   ★

They held the coroner's inquest the next day in the courthouse. Sheriff Spears was also coroner; he presided. It did not take long. The jury consisted of six men.

When the evidence was in the jury went out. But instead of debating, they sat around the table and drank hard whisky. Finally the bailiff stuck in his head.

'Got your verdict yet?'

'Yes.'

Ed Cotton was sitting in the front row with Connie Wilford. Big Jim had testified he had not lost a horse; he had lent the two stolen horses, he had lied, to Ed Cotton and to Booger Sam.

His daughter had made him say it.

Sheriff Spears asked, 'Jury, your verdict?'

The foreman stood up with difficulty. The hard whisky had hit him in the belly. His voice was thick.

'Nobody is guilty of nothin' an' them defendants is free to roam the country an' live like men, not like hunted cold animals.

184

Everybody is free of everythin', Sheriff.'

He tried to sit down, and he almost missed the chair. Booger Sam, smiling widely, looked at Ed Cotton.

'Now we can go out to your spread an' do the chores, Edward.'

Ed Cotton got to his feet. He had a sudden thought: Next door lay two bodies, cold in the morgue. Downing and Rome would steal no more furs; nor would they ever again cut another fence. Beside them lay two other bodies—two trappers Downing had murdered.

This thought was not good.

He looked down at Connie. She had tears in her eyes. He looked back at Booger Sam.

'You're not doin' chores with me today, Booger.'

Booger Sam looked at him. 'Why?'

Ed looked again at Connie, who now stood beside him. All eyes were on him; all ears heard his words.

'Connie and me are goin' to do those chores.'

Photoset, printed and bound in Great Britain by
REDWOOD BURN LIMITED, Trowbridge, Wiltshire